Aurélia : Sylvie

Gérard de Nerval

Gérard de Nerval

Aurélia

•

followed by

•

Sylvie

Translated by

•

KENDALL LAPPIN

With an Introduction and Notes by

•

ERIC BASSO

Santa Maria • Asylum Arts • 1993

Acknowledgements

Aurélia translation Copyright © 1991 by Kendall Lappin
Sylvie translation Copyright © 1993 by Kendall Lappin
Introduction and notes to *Aurélia* Copyright © 1991 by Eric Basso
Notes to *Sylvie* Copyright © 1993 by Eric Basso

Library of Congress Catalog Number 90-83544
ISBN No. 1-878580-07-8

Cover photograph by Anne Arden McDonald.

Asylum Arts Publishing
P. O. Box 6203
Santa Maria, CA 93456

Contents

Aurélia / Sylvie

INTRODUCTION

The Heart in Winter

"Do you remember when we went out in that filthy weather to see the place where Gérard de Nerval hanged himself?" That's Anna Deslions, a courtesan, speaking two years after the fact to an actress, one Juliette Beau, on the topic of suicide. The Goncourt brothers are present at this intimate dinner party, which has something of a brothel atmosphere about it. In their famous *Journal*, Anna is described as a financier's "former mistress" and "the woman who ruined" the Comte de Lauriston, an aide-de-camp to Napoleon III. And Juliette? A "little blonde with something of the Rosalba picture in the Louvre, *Woman with Monkey*, partaking of the monkey as well as the woman." She recalls the event: "Yes, and I even believe it was you who paid for the cab. I touched the bar; it was that that brought me luck." Both the Goncourts and those of the *beau monde* who made their morbid, but typically Parisian, pilgrimage to the site of Gérard's demise would have thought him one more casualty of the *mal du siècle*, yet another minor Romantic poet, an old curiosity, come to a bad end. This view, reinforced by the well-intentioned eulogies and reminiscences of Nerval's friends, persisted for nearly seventy years until the Surrealists and members of the *Grand Jeu* group undertook a long-overdue reappraisal of the life and works. But between Gérard's death in 1855 and his belated "rehabilitation," the familiar anecdotes prevailed. Théophile Gautier, who had known the deceased since their student days at the Lycée Charlemagne, pictures the young Nerval walking around Paris with his head in the clouds, his pockets stuffed with scraps of unfinished poems, essays, dramas, and any books and pamphlets he happened to be reading. The poet's translation of *Faust* (published in 1827, when Gérard was nineteen) aroused the admiration of Goethe himself who, Gautier assures us, "had deigned to say that he had never so well understood his own work" as in this new French version. In his *Confessions*, Arsène Houssaye says Gérard "kept [his father] at a distance for two reasons: first, because he believed himself to be the son of Napoleon; and second because [his father] had thrown his first verses into the fire with many angry words against all poets." The most famous "legend" concerning Nerval's extravagant ideas and behavior may actually be true. During his last years, Gautier spotted him in the Palais Royal dragging a lobster along on a blue-ribbon leash. Nerval told his friend he saw nothing odd about his pet crustacean: "I like lobsters; they are quiet, serious, know the secrets of the sea, don't bark and don't swallow people's monads as do dogs, so repugnant to Goethe, who surely was not crazy." Another crony, Jules Husson Champfleury, reports a conversation Gérard held with some goldfish swimming in a pond of the Tuileries Gardens. "The Queen of Sheba awaits you," said the fish. Nerval told Champfleury he declined the royal invitation because he "didn't wish to offend Solomon's vanity." We shall come upon the Queen of Sheba again, for she has many faces.

Nerval's friends are all agreed upon his amiability, his spellbinding conversation, his generosity and his inveterate wanderings. In the early days, when Nerval shared a small apartment not far from the Louvre on the Impasse du Doyenné with Camille Rogier, Houssaye and Gautier he was hardly ever seen there. Houssaye calls him "a very easy tenant because he never slept at home." Now and again, Gérard would drop in for an hour or two during the day. "In the evening he went to the theater and during the night he prowled about totally absorbed by the fever of inspiration. When these struggles had wearied him he lay down to sleep wherever he happened to be." He said nothing to his roommates of these nocturnal ramblings, preferring to keep them a mystery; they were simply a part of his method, the means by which he worked, for it seems he could write almost anywhere, except perhaps at a desk in a comfortable room. But there was another side to Gérard de Nerval that his friends failed to bring out in their memoirs. They harked back to the eccentricities of his youth and saw there the germ of the madness which would come to destroy him. Excuses had to be made, an explanation found. With the benefit of hindsight, Gautier, Houssaye and others came to view the half-dozen escapades attributed to the young Gérard (none so out-of-the-ordinary when one recalls the activities of Borel "the Lycanthrope" and other French Romantics of the time) as the root cause of the insanity that had robbed them of their beloved friend. To them, his fall seemed predestined. Yet Nerval's own writings and letters reveal quite a different man. His father was a military doctor, and he himself a medical student. During the terrible cholera epidemic of 1832, Gérard helped his father to care for the sick and the dying; it was a time of mass graves, of corpses piled high for burning—to the survivors it appeared as though the world were coming to an end, and the young poet witnessed at first hand the agonies of over a hundred victims. Under such conditions one has little time to be a solitary dreamer; even so, Nerval had already completed and published many of the *Odelettes* (Little Odes), his first major cycle of poems, in various literary journals. Chief amongst Gérard's private pursuits was the study of ancient rites and religions, classical and occult mythologies, the Tarot and the Kabbalah; his tireless erudition embraced German poetry and fiction, French literature's obscurist byways from medieval to "modern" times, and the works of Shakespeare, Swift, Sterne and Dickens. The strange philosophy of his sonnet, "Vers dorés" (Golden Verses, published 1845), anticipated Victor Hugo's longer Pythagorian poem, "Ce que dit la Bouche d'ombre" (Words from the Mouth of Darkness), by nearly a decade. Throughout most of his life Nerval seems to have enjoyed a robust health. He traveled widely on and off the European continent, and never felt more at home than when he set foot in some foreign land. It matters little that the "Orient" he created from his travels in the Middle East owed perhaps too much to his imagination when he came to write the book of his journey there; what counts more for us now, as we look at Gérard's biography and try to pierce the smokescreen of misbegotten lore thrown up by those who thought they knew him well, is the evidence of an existence rich in human experience. He was nowhere near unworldly, as we had been given to believe. In *Gérard de Nerval: The Mystic's Dilemma*, Bettina L. Knapp points out that Nerval's attitude to so-called "mystical" and "psychic" phenomena was "always ambivalent." Indeed, Gérard's letters often reveal his skepticism, though at other times he appears to be a believer. His first real exposure to books took place when he was a child living in his uncle's house at Mortefontaine. Among the "huge mass of books piled up and forgotten in the garret" were a number of tomes dating from the French Revolution. Here Nerval discovered not only Rousseau and those *excentriques* like Cazotte and Restif whose life stories he would recount (and sometimes reinvent) in *Les Illuminés* (Luminaries), but also undoubtedly the works of Voltaire. Yet, as he grew older, and the terrible mental crises he sustained inclined him toward a search for what he had lost by seeking signs of wonder in the most innocuous incidents and places, Nerval's occult readings returned with a vengeance to guide him through the endless labyrinth of his waking nightmare. At the heart of the maze stood a ghost, the figure of a woman whose remembrance had driven him

iv

insane. The madness would provide him with the substance of a dream made flesh and an extraordinary personal document that has become a classic of French prose, *Aurélia*.

Books of dreams and madness, Gérard de Nerval's is only one of many. In 1867, Hervey de Saint-Denys, a Sinologist at the Collège de France who had been recording his dreams since childhood, published *Les Rêves et les moyens de les diriger* (How to Control Dreams), based on his own experiences and researches, the most thorough treatment of the subject to appear before Freud carried it one step further into the realm of symbolic interpretation at the turn of the century. An anonymous eighteenth-century author had promised to teach his readers how to be "happy" in dreams by fulfilling their innnermost desires—Gérard may well have come across this one in his uncle's abandoned library. Swedenborg, the theosophist whose ideas would come to influence both Balzac and the French Romantics, kept a dream diary, and the British poet Robert Southey religiously inscribed his nightmares in his *Commonplace Books*. Michel Leiris and René Daumal wrote extensively on dreams and, along with the Surrealists, conducted their own experiments in the unconscious. More recently Michel Butor, Henri Gougaud, François Damian and Robert Nye have concocted books out of both real and imaginary dreams. Of those who went insane and either recorded their experiences during lucid intervals or simply gave expression to their madness through their works, the poets Friedrich Hölderlin and John Clare come immediately to mind. August Strindberg left a powerful account of his days and nights as a mad scientist at the sinister Hôtel Orfila in 1890s Paris; his *Inferno* was written in French. Some twenty years later the ballet dancer Nijinsky would write the diary of his own descent into schizophrenia, to be followed not long after by Antonin Artaud's anatomy of mental paralysis in a classic series of letters to the critic

Jacques Rivière. The field of study is rich. From madness we
return to dreams and the book Nerval held to be the closest
in spirit to his *Aurélia*. Francesco Colonna published the
Hypnerotomachia Poliphili (Poliphilo's Dream) in 1499;
written in a combination of Italian and Latin, with Greek
inscriptions and woodcut illustrations, this curious incunabulum was translated into French in 1546. Nerval refers
to it in the introduction to his *Voyage en Orient* as providing
"some curious details about the cult of the heavenly Venus
on the Isle of Cythera." Gérard recounts how the impover-
ished painter Colonna fell madly in love with the Principessa Lucrezia Polia of Treviso. She returned his love, but
as an orphan of lowly origin Colonna could never hope to
marry a woman of rank. He became a Dominican friar and
she retired to a nunnery. If they could not be together in life,
they were determined to dream of each other, of the happier
existence they might have had. Colonna's book is the record
of the trials he endured in his slumbers, a long, oneiric poem
of love to the woman whose body he was forced to renounce.
In the last of his dreams, Poliphilo (Colonna) and Polia are
united in a mystical marriage under the sign of Venus at
Cythera. Some of the book's early French commentators
claimed they detected a complex web of alchemical symbols
underlying the text, an aspect of the work which would not
have escaped Nerval even without their "learned" glosses.
But what Gérard most admired was Francesco Colonna's
dedication to renouncement. By his devotion to the "cult" of
Lucrezia Polia, to which the *Hypnerotomachia* served as a
New Testament, the Italian painter-turned-monk gave
comfort and guidance to Nerval in his own dark winter of
loss. Yet to make of a woman an object of private worship,
flattering though it may be, is to deny her existence in and
of itself, to create a goddess, a madonna, a sacred whore, a
Queen of Sheba whose true face must remain forever veiled,
for to reveal it would be to uncover the face of Death, the
annihilation of the worshipper. Not only did Gérard plan, in

the very month of his death, to write a play entitled *Francesco Colonna*, but through one of those providential coincidences that seemed to crop up everywhere during the closing decade of his life the name of the author of *Poliphilo's Dream* became inextricably linked with the woman who stood at the vortex of his personal tragedy. An early version of Nerval's sonnet to "Myrtho", whom he calls a "divine enchantress" with "golden hair," is dedicated "to J-y Colonna." Who was she?

In the chapters of *Les Illuminés* dealing with the life and loves of the eighteenth-century printer-novelist Restif de la Bretonne, Nerval cautions us: "Nothing is more dangerous for those with a natural tendency to be dreamers than a serious love for a person of the theater; it is a perpetual lie, a sick man's dream, a madman's illusion. Life attaches itself completely to an unrealizable chimera, which one would be happy to preserve in its state of desire and aspiration, but which vanishes as soon as one tries to touch the idol." Scholars are not in agreement about when Gérard de Nerval first laid eyes upon Jenny Colon; some say 1833, others 1834. She was a *comédienne* (an actress who also sang in operettas) appearing in such theaters as the Gymnase, the Opéra-Comique and the Variétés, by all accounts a woman of exquisite looks and bearing, with a voluptuous figure and a captivating voice. Nerval, hard, but pleasantly, at work as a drama critic, seems to have fallen for her immediately, and returned each night to see her performance at the Variétés. He admired her from afar, sending her flowers anonymously. Months were to pass before he summoned up the courage to introduce himself to her. During the next two years Nerval would squander the remains of an inheritance left to him by his maternal grandfather by founding *Le Monde dramatique*, a sumptuous magazine whose main purpose was to further the career of Jenny Colon. That he and she were the same age convinced him their love was predestined. Exactly what transpired between them? No one knows. In an age remarkable for backstairs gossip and the scabrous anecdote (one has merely to consult the Goncourt *Journal*) Gérard's closest friends displayed an uncharacteristic discretion on the subject of his relations with the alluring *comédienne*; this curious silence is the measure of a loyalty unheard-of at the time, an indication of the degree to which Nerval's memory inspired an almost brotherly protection in those who survived him. Disparate theories have been advanced to explain the "fault" for which the narrator of *Aurélia* seeks forgiveness, an act, rightly or wrongly, seen by many as the key to the nature of Gérard's liaison with Jenny. L.-H. Sébillotte contends that Nerval was impotent (at least with a woman like Jenny Colon, who meant so much to him); others tender the view that the poet's sexual escapades with other women caused him to feel unworthy of the idealized Jenny or that, having fashioned her into the Idol, the reality of the human being became more than he could bear, a sort of living, breathing contradiction to his cherished fantasy. An even more intriguing hypothesis, set forth by Jean Sennelier in *Un Amour inconnu de Gérard de Nerval* (Gérard de Nerval's Unknown Love), throws our protagonist into the arms of another actress, the luscious Esther de Bongars, at about the time he had fallen in love with Jenny, this based upon information provided by an actor who knew them both and referred to their "unusual love relationship." The strange *Lettres à Aurélia* (Letters to Aurelia, not titled by Nerval), believed by some to have been written from three to four years after his first meeting with Jenny, only serve to further obscure the matter, for though the manuscript variants to letter IV do suggest that Jenny Colon was indeed Gérard's mistress, Nerval later crossed them out; they may, or may not, have been fictional elaborations. Whatever truly occurred between them, one can only agree with Bettina Knapp that "nothing real seemed to have come from [Nerval's] relationship with Jenny Colon," and the labors he put himself to on her behalf—his libretto *La Reine de Saba* (The Queen of Sheba, passively rejected by Meyerbeer), his collaboration with Dumas *père* on *Piquillo* (a critical failure), and the short play *Corilla* (never performed)—also came to very little. In 1838, less than a year after her appearance in *Piquillo*, Jenny Colon married her tour manager, the flutist Louis-Marie-Gabriel Leplus. Gérard seems to have taken the blow philosophically. Perhaps he was unconsciously relieved by the knowledge that Jenny's marriage now placed her definitively beyond his grasp, though what we know of the mores of Louis Philippe's Paris makes a mockery of such matrimonial "virtue." Nevertheless, as if to confirm his delusion, Jenny appears to have been a faithful wife, dutifully presenting her flutist with children while Nerval descended into another world in search of her ghost. Four years after her wedding (worn out by her pregnancies, some say), Jenny Colon died. Gérard saw her for the last time in Brussels on the occasion of her appearance in a revival of *Piquillo*. There the poet sustained the shock of finding himself between the two women who meant the most to him, for the beautiful pianist Marie Pleyel had arranged the meeting, which took place at her home. It was too much for him. Not long after his return to Paris, Nerval suffered his first mental breakdown.

Marie Pleyel was famous. In her time, she had turned the heads of many men; Berlioz and Mendelssohn were among their number, and Gérard de Nerval. Her musical talent and physical allure are incontestable. Gérard met her toward the close of 1839 in Vienna, where he had come to seek some diversion after the failure of his plays *Leo Burckhart* and *The Alchemist* (the latter written with the collaboration of Dumas *père*). As a distraction from his loss of Jenny Colon, Marie Pleyel could not have been more suitable, for her dark beauty and raven hair were not calculated to remind him of the blonde *comédienne*. The fact that Marie was accomplished, charming, beautiful, already married, and *not* Jenny, must have made her irresistible. The nature of Nerval's relations with Marie Pleyel remains a mystery, one furthered by the novella *Pandora*, which he loosely based on his Viennese adventures. Marie's charm and beauty survive in *Pandora*, but her fictional counterpart is a sadistic vamp, a she-demon, a fickle temptress. This story of love and betrayal ends in a fever of madness; the narrator, comparing his fate to that of Prometheus, tells us he can still feel the beak of the vulture tearing into his flesh, and prays to the god Jupiter for his deliverance. Clearly, Marie Pleyel little resembled the dangerous Pandora. Her letters prove she was genuinely fond of Nerval, and the arrangement of his meeting with Jenny Colon can only be taken as an act of kindness; she could not have foreseen the disastrous effect it would have on the poet. The Kafkaesque *Pandora*, written over a decade after the event by a man whose hold upon "reality" had come to be precarious at best, may well have been an act of revenge.

In 1840, the very year Nerval last set eyes on Jenny Colon (such coincidences were always of capital importance to him), there died a woman whose image had haunted him almost since childhood: Sophie Dawes, the mysterious Baronne de Feuchères. She had been the English mistress of the Prince de Condé. After the Restoration, the aged Prince returned with her to France, passed her off as his illegitimate daughter, and talked Adrien de Feuchères into marrying her by offering to make him a baron and bestowing a large dowry upon the bride. Sometime after the marriage, the new Baron de Feuchères learned the truth about his wife and the Prince, and was granted a separation. In 1827, the Prince de Condé purchased the castle of Mortefontaine for Sophie; there, on his daily walk, young Gérard often saw the elegant horsewoman riding through her estate, the vision of a lovely but distant amazon. When the Prince was found hanged from the bolt of his bedroom window three years later, it did not look like suicide—his feet touched the ground, the handkerchief around his neck was slack. Many suspected the Baronne de Feuchères of complicity in his murder, for since their return from England she had been leading him a merry dance; the case came to trial, but the charges against her were dismissed. Some claimed the old lecher had died of accidental strangulation while attempting to revive his flagging sexual ardor. Gérard certainly knew of the sinister rumors surrounding the Baroness. He almost certainly did not know that Sophie Dawes, a fisherman's daughter, had risen from a life of whoring and the theater to become the entrancing Baronne de Feuchères. Because she was a woman whom he always saw at a distance, who remained at one remove in life and death, she maintained her position as the first and "purest" of the models upon which Nerval would construct his masterpiece. And so, at the end of that fatal year of 1840, Gérard de Nerval hurried back from Brussels to Paris. The Baronne de Feuchéres was dead. Jenny Colon and Marie Pleyel survived as reminders of his own living desolation. He spoke to his friends of an "imperious duty," of a debt to be paid. Two months later, overwhelmed by the obligation of having taken on twice as much journalistic work as before in order to keep his head above water, he became more and more isolated; then came the hallucinations, vivid dreams and waking visions of his long-dead mother, of Jenny, Marie, the Baroness and other women—now at last he took possession of them all, they were his alone. On February 23, 1841, in the midst of Mardi Gras celebrations on the Rue Miromesnil, terrified by costumed revelers whose masks looked to him like breathing gargoyles, he began to take off his clothes as if to rid himself of the layers of chains which seemed to hold him rooted to the spot. He felt an "electricity" flowing through his veins; certain of his invincibility, he fought off a man who tried to subdue him. The night watch seized him, and he was led off to the nearest police station. The next day, they interned him in a rest home. The doctors diagnosed his condition: schizophrenia marked by intervals of aphasia and cataleptic exhaustion. Twelve years later, the condition recurred. From then until the time of his death, Gérard de Nerval would be in and out of mental clinics; sometimes he'd grow stuporous and withdrawn, at other times so violent that sharp or potentially dangerous objects had to be removed from his room. His creative powers seemed actually to increase during those prolonged periods of lucidity which enabled him to function in society and even to resume his travels. Thus he continued to live, surrounded by unseen threats at every turn and a prey to chaos.

At about the end of 1853, Dr. Emile Blanche, director of the progressive clinic for the mentally ill at Passy (and son of the Dr. Blanche who first looked after Gérard in 1841), encouraged his patient to set down an account of his dreams and visions for therapeutic reasons. Some scholars, however, believe that *Aurélia* was begun as early as 1841 and worked on sporadically until December 1853, at which time the real writing commenced; others maintain Nerval began *Aurélia* in earnest the following year, 1854, during his last trip to Germany. It no longer seems right to regard *Aurélia* as "unfinished." Again, we must lay the blame for yet another misunderstanding at the feet of Gérard's well-meaning friends. In the 1855 edition, edited by Gautier and Houssaye, this note appears after the final sentence: "This is Gérard de Nerval's last page. Here the poet's pen was broken, the golden pen of feeling and imagination." But as Henri Lemaitre points out in a modern edition of the work, the author returns, at the very end, to his opening theme— the dream as "a second life"—and maintains, as throughout the narrative, the "double reference to Christianity and Antiquity." Thus, the formal structure of Nerval's "descent into hell" is complete; the last words return us to the first, and this long prose poem closes in upon itself even as it opens outward toward the promise of a new life. *Aurélia* is

the haunting by Nerval of the women who haunted him—
Jenny Colon above all, but also Marie Pleyel and the Baronne de Feuchères. Whereas the latter two became emblems
of the demonic and the mysterious respectively, in Jenny
these qualities merged and were absorbed in the angelic
image of the mother Gérard had lost as a child. Jenny
Colon's death was her transfiguration into the goddess, the
Madonna through whom the poet would seek his salvation,
and also the Eurydice, symbol of a glowing past, of a loss
which could only be recovered by a harrowing journey
through the nether world. All the major commentators on
Aurélia have recognized this. Yet René Daumal ends his
essay, "Nerval le nyctalope" (1930), by stating that the other
side of Aurélia's Eternal Feminine is Lilith—coldness, ste-
rility, the void. The Queen of Sheba dropped her masks one
by one until the freezing midwinter morning when Gérard
de Nerval passed into the narrow cul-de-sac of the Rue
Basse de la Vieille-Lanterne, drew an ecru-colored rope he
thought to have belonged to Madame de Maintenon around
the bar of a vent hole above the street (the bar Juliette Beau
would touch for luck), and hanged himself. Only after he had
stared into the face behind the last of the dread Queen's veils
did he see the *impossibility* of it all. Anteros, the god of
unrequited love, can find no rest but in annihilation. Under
this sign the tormented Berlioz wooed his ideal woman into
a disastrous marriage, and the mad daughter of Victor Hugo
crossed the ocean to shadow the British lieutenant whom
she imagined to be her husband. Nerval's failure with Jenny
Colon led him to recreate her in an impossible image; during
his last hours, she was as lost to him in death as she had been
in life. In *Sylvie*, he recognized his love for the captivating
comédienne as "vague and hopeless." In *Les Illuminés*, he
wrote that unrequited love is tolerable only until the age of
forty; thereafter, a man "suffers doubly from these affec-
tions and from his outraged dignity."

"One of us was once in love for eight days with a woman

of fairly easy virtue, and the other for three days with a ten-franc whore. Altogether, eleven days of love between the two of us." It's the Goncourts again, writing nine years after Gérard de Nerval's suicide. One cannot help but think he might have envied them. Today we know the name of Jenny Colon only because he loved her. In *Voyage en Orient* he would say, almost in passing, "It was not enough for me to have put my loves of flesh and those of ashes into the tomb to assure myself that it is we, the living, who walk in a world of phantoms."

— Eric Basso
November 1987

Aurélia

$\mathcal{T}$HE $\mathcal{D}$REAM is a second life. Never can I pass without a shudder through those gates of ivory or horn which separate us from the invisible world. The first moments of sleep are the counterpart of death: a kind of nebulous sluggishness paralyzes our thinking, and at some instant which we cannot precisely determine, the *self*, in another form, continues the work of our existence. This is a kind of subterranean realm which is gradually illumined, and where the pale, grave, immobile figures who inhabit the land of limbo emerge from shadows and darkness. Then the tableau takes form, and a new kind of light illuminates and sets in motion these bizarre apparitions; the world of the Spirits is opening to us.

Swedenborg[1] called his visions *Memorabilia*; he used to have them more often in reverie than in sleep; Apuleius'[2] *The Golden Ass* and Dante's *The Divine Comedy* are the poetic models of these studies of the human soul. Following their example, I shall attempt to transcribe my impressions of a lingering malady which has run its course entirely

---

[1]Emanuel Swedenborg (1688-1772), Swedish philosopher, scientist, mystic. Extremely influential on such writers as Balzac, Gautier and Nerval. Kept a diary of his dreams and visions.

[2]Apuleius of Madaura (born ca. 114 A. D.), author of *The Golden Ass*, a satirical autobiography. Transformed into an ass by mistake, the protagonist observes the follies and vices of his various masters until the goddess Isis returns him to his human form.

within the mysterious confines of my mind; yet I do not know why I use the term "malady," for so far as I myself am concerned, I have never felt healthier. At times I have felt that my strength and energy were doubled; I have seemed to know everything, comprehend everything; imagination has brought me infinite delights. When I recover what men call my reason, shall I be obliged to regret having lost these pleasures?

This *Vita Nuova*[3] of mine has consisted of two phases. Here are the notes dealing with the first phase. — A lady whom I had been in love with for a long time, and whom I shall call Aurelia, was lost to me. The circumstances of this loss, which was to affect my life so greatly, are not important. Every reader can search his own memory for his greatest heartbreak, the most crushing blow ever dealt his soul by fate, after which he had to resolve whether to die or go on living; — I shall explain later why I did not choose death. Condemned by the woman I loved, guilty of a transgression for which I no longer had any hope of being forgiven, I had no recourse save to throw myself into the pursuit of vulgar pleasures; I affected happiness and insouciance; I traveled a great deal, madly enamored of variety and caprice; I especially enjoyed seeing the strange costumes, customs and behavior of people in distant lands, for it seemed to me that I was thereby displacing the conditions of good and evil—the terms, as it were, of what constitutes *feeling* for us Frenchmen. "What madness," I kept telling myself, "to go on loving platonically a woman who no longer loves you. My reading is to blame for all this; I have taken

---

[3] *La Vita Nuova* (1290-94), by Dante: a cycle of thirty-one poems, linked by commentaries in prose, having mainly to do with the poet's love for the unattainable Beatrice.

seriously the contrivances of poets, and have made a Laura[4] or a Beatrice for myself out of an ordinary, contemporary person . . . So let's pass on to other love affairs, and this one will soon be forgotten." The joyous whirl of a carnival season in a certain Italian city drove all melancholy thoughts from my mind. I was so glad to be feeling thus relieved that I informed all my friends of my happiness, and gave them to understand, in my letters, that this was my habitual state of mind, when in reality it was nothing more than a feverish excess of excitement.

One day there arrived in that city a certain woman of great prominence who took a liking to me and who, being experienced at pleasing and dazzling men, quite easily lured me into the circle of her admirers. After an evening during which she had been so natural and so charming that all of us were greatly impressed, I felt so captivated by her that I could not resist the urge to write her a letter at once. I was so happy to feel my heart capable of a new love! In this state of artificial enthusiasm, I employed in my letter the very same verbal expressions which had served me, such a short time before, to declare a genuine, time-tested love. Having posted the letter, I wished I had not done so; and I went off to ponder in solitude what seemed to me a profanation of my memories.

Evening restored to my new love all its previous glamor. The lady expressed her appreciation of what I had written, together with a degree of surprise at my sudden fervor. I had passed through, in a single day, several stages of the feelings a man can have for a woman with any likelihood of their being sincere. She confessed that I had astonished her, but

---

[4]Laura, the Italian poet Petrarch's ideal love. Through marriage, an ancestor of the Marquis de Sade.

said I had also made her very proud. I attempted to convince her of my sincerity; but no matter what I tried to say to her, I was unable in our subsequent meetings to recapture the tone of what I had written, so that in the end I was obliged to confess to her, tearfully, that I had not only treated her badly but had deceived myself as well. My emotional confidences, however, did have a certain charm; and my vain protestations of love were succeeded by a firm friendship between us, all the stronger for its lenity.

II

Later, I encountered her again in another city where the lady with whom I was still hopelessly in love was residing. By chance the two became acquainted, and the former must have had occasion to speak of me, moving to pity the one who had banished me from her heart. So one day, finding myself at a gathering where my true love was also present, I saw her come toward me and extend her hand. How was I to interpret this action and the look of profound melancholy with which she greeted me? I thought I saw in it forgiveness for the past; the divine accent of pity imparted to the simple words she spoke to me a value beyond words, as if something of a religious nature was being added to the sweetness of a hitherto secular love, and was setting upon it the seal of eternity.

An urgent business matter obliged me to return to Paris; but I quickly resolved to stay there only a few days, then to hurry back to my two sweethearts. Joy and impatience made my head swim, and this was complicated by a feeling of anxiety about the business I had to conclude. One evening, about midnight, I was walking up the street toward my lodgings when, raising my eyes by chance, I noticed a house-number illuminated by a street-lamp. The number was that of my age. Immediately thereafter, upon lowering my eyes, I saw before me a pale, hollow-eyed woman who seemed to have Aurelia's features. I said to myself: "It is *her death*, or my own, that I am being given notice of!" But for some reason I settled on the latter supposition, and the idea struck me that this was going to happen the following day at the same hour.

That night I had a dream which confirmed this thought in my mind. — I was wandering through a huge building composed of a number of large rooms, some being used as classrooms, others devoted to conversation or philosophical discussion. Interested, I entered one of the classrooms, where I thought I recognized my former teachers and fellow-students. The lessons, on Greek and Latin writers, went droning on in that murmuring monotone that seems like a prayer to the goddess Mnemosyne.[5] — Then I went on into another room, where some philosophical lectures were taking place. After taking part in this for a while, I went off to find my room in a sort of hostelry with immense stair-cases, crowded with bustling travelers.

I lost my way several times in the long corridors, and upon crossing one of the central galleries, I was confronted by a strange spectacle. A winged being of tremendous size—man or woman, I couldn't tell—was hovering laboriously overhead, and seemed to be floundering about in dense clouds. Weakened and short of breath, it finally fell into the center of the dark inner courtyard, its wings catching and scraping along rooftops and balusters. I managed to get a brief look at it. Its coloring was in shades of bright red, and its wings shimmered with a thousand changing reflections.

---

[5]Mnemosyne, the Greek goddess of memory. Mother of the nine Muses.

Clad in a long robe with classical folds, it resembled Albrecht Dürer's Angel in *Melancholia*.[6]— I cried out involuntarily in terror, waking myself up with a start.

The next day, I made haste to call on all my friends. I said my goodbyes to them mentally, and without telling them what was preying on my mind, I discoursed enthusiastically and authoritatively on mystical subjects; I surprised them with a peculiar eloquence; it seemed to me that I knew everything, that in these, my final hours on earth, the mysteries of the world were being revealed to me.

That evening when the fatal hour seemed to be approaching, I was sitting with two friends at a club table, holding forth on painting and music, defining my point of view on the generation of colors and the meaning of numbers. One of the friends, Paul _____ by name, offered to walk me back to my lodgings, but I told him I wasn't going home. "Where are you going?" he asked. — *"To the East!"* And with him in my company, I began to search the sky for a certain star I thought I knew, as though it had some bearing on my destiny. Having found it, I set off again, choosing streets whose direction enabled me to keep the star in view, — marching, as it were, to meet my fate, and determined not to lose sight of that star until the very moment when death was to strike me. Upon coming to the confluence of three streets, however, I refused to go any farther. It seemed to me that my friend was exerting a superhuman force upon me to keep me moving; to my eyes he was growing taller in stature and was taking on the look of an apostle. I seemed to see the spot where we were standing rise into the air and lose the forms given it by its urban configuration; — now high on a hill, surrounded by a vast, lonely wilderness, this spot was

---

[6]Dürer's engraving *Melancholia* depicts a sullen angel whose room, cluttered with symbolic objects, overlooks a gloomy bayside city.

becoming a scene of combat between two Spirits, like a Biblical temptation. "No!" I said. "Thy Heaven is not for me. Within that star are the souls who are awaiting me. They are anterior to the revelation Thou hast made to me. Let me join them, for the woman I love is among them, and that is where we shall be reunited!"

III

Here began for me what I shall call the overflowing of the dream into real life. From this moment on, everything took on at times a dual aspect, and this without the reasoning process ever lacking logic, without memory losing the slightest detail of what was happening to me. But my actions, apparently those of a madman, were subject to what human reason would call illusion.

Many times this idea has occurred to me: that at certain crucial moments in my life, this or that Spirit from the outer world has incarnated itself in the body of some ordinary person to influence or attempt to influence me, without that person's being aware of it or remembering it afterward.

My friend had left me, seeing that his efforts to calm me were useless, and no doubt thinking that if I walked long enough, the obsession I was under would pass. Finding myself alone, I got to my feet with some difficulty and set off again in the direction of the star, keeping my eyes fixed constantly upon it. As I walked along, I sang a mysterious hymn which I seemed to remember having heard in some other existence and which filled me with an ineffable joy. Meanwhile I began taking off my earthly garments and scattering them around me. The route seemed to lead ever upward, and the star to become larger and larger. Then I stopped, with my arms extended, awaiting the moment when the soul would leave my body and be drawn magnetically into the beam of the star. A shudder came over me: regret at leaving the earth and the persons in it whom I loved clutched at my heart, and inwardly I beseeched so ardently the Spirit who was drawing me to him, that it seemed I was descending again to the world of men. I found myself encircled by a night-watch patrol; — at that point I felt that I had become very tall, and so heavily charged with electrical power that I would be sure to destroy whoever or whatever came near me. There was something comical about the care I took to keep my powers in check and to spare the lives of the soldiers who had collected me.

If I did not believe it to be the mission of a writer to analyze honestly what he feels and experiences at crucial times in his life, and if I did not have, in doing so, a purpose that I believe to be useful, I would stop here, and would not attempt to describe what happened to me thereafter in a series of visions, perhaps due to insanity or to some commonplace illness. Lying on a cot, I seemed to see the heavens unveiled and opened, revealing a thousand vistas of unparalleled magnificence. It seemed that the destiny of the liberated Soul was being revealed to me, as if to make me regret having willed with all my might to regain a foothold on this earth which I was about to depart... Immense circles were traced in the infinite, like the spherical shapes water takes when it is displaced by a falling body; each separate region, peopled by radiant figures, took on color, moved, then dissolved in its turn; and a female Deity, always the same one, smilingly removed, one after another, the fleeting masks of her various incarnations, and finally disappeared, inscrutable, into the mystic splendors of the sky of Asia.

This celestial vision, by one of those phenomena which everyone has experienced in certain dreams, did not keep me from being fully aware of everything that was going on around me. Lying on a cot, I heard the soldiers talking about an unidentified individual, under arrest like me, whose voice had echoed in that very room. By an odd effect of sympathetic vibration, it seemed to me that that voice was resonating within my breast, and that my soul was somehow being split in two, divided cleanly between vision and reality. For an instant I thought about turning around abruptly to face that person they were discussing; then with a shudder I remembered a tradition, widespread in Germany, which says that every man has a *double*, and that when he sees him, death is imminent. I closed my eyes and lapsed into a confused state of mind in which the figures around me, real or imaginary, broke up into a thousand fleeting images. At one moment, I saw close at hand two friends of mine coming to get me, and the soldiers pointing me out; then the door opened, and someone just my size, whose face I could not see, went out with my friends, whom I tried vainly to call back. "You're making a mistake!" I shouted. "I'm the one they came for, and it's someone else who's leaving!" I raised such a row that they locked me in a cell.

I remained there for several hours in a kind of brutish stupor; finally, the two friends whom I *thought* I had seen earlier arrived, in a carriage, to get me. I told them everything that had occurred, but they denied having come there during the night. I dined with them tranquilly enough, but as night approached, it seemed to me that I had reason to dread the exact hour which had so nearly been my last, the night before. I asked one of them to give me an Oriental ring he had on his finger, which I regarded as an ancient talisman; and running a foulard through the ring, I tied it around my neck, being careful to place the setting, a turquoise, against a certain point on the nape, where I felt a pain. I was certain that this was the point at which my soul might leave my body, if and when a certain ray of light from the star I had seen the previous night should happen to coincide with the zenith directly above my head. Whether by chance or as a result of my intense preoccupation, I collapsed as if struck by lightning—at the exact same time as on the previous night. They laid me on a bed, and for a long time I could not determine the meaning nor the interrelationship of the images which presented themselves to me. This condition lasted several days. I was taken to a hospital. A number of relatives and friends came there to visit me, without my being aware of their presence. For me the only difference between waking and sleeping was that when I was awake, everything was transfigured to my eyes; every person who approached me seemed transformed, material objects had about them a kind of penumbra which altered their shape, and light-refractions and color-combinations were distorted, so that I was subjected to a continuous series of overlapping impressions; and when I was asleep, the absence of external elements in my dreams maintained the plausibility of these impressions.

IV

One evening, I was certain I had been transported to the banks of the Rhine. Across from me were some sinister-looking rocks, their outline etched darkly against the sky. I entered a cheerful house with the rays of the setting sun shining through its green shutters festooned with grapevines. I seemed to be coming back to a familiar dwelling, the house of a maternal uncle of mine, a Flemish painter, dead for more than a century. Some rough sketches of his paintings were hung here and there; one of them represented the celebrated fairy of this waterside. An old servant, whom I addressed as Marguerite and whom it seemed I had known since childhood, said to me: "Why don't you go lie down on the bed for a while? You've come a long way, and your uncle won't be home until late. We'll wake you when supper is ready." I lay down on a four-poster whose chintz bedspread had big red flowers on it. On the wall opposite me hung a rustic wooden clock, and on that clock sat a bird which began to talk to me like a person. I perceived that the soul of one of my ancestors was in that clock; but I was no more surprised by its form and its speech than I was to find myself seemingly transported backward in time by a hundred years. The bird spoke to me about persons in my family, persons who were still living or had died at different times in the past, as if they all existed simultaneously, and said to me: "You can see that your uncle took care to paint *her* portrait in advance . . . she is now with us." I turned to look at a canvas showing a woman dressed in the old German style, bending over a stream, with her eyes fixed on a clump of forget-me-nots. Meanwhile darkness was gradually falling, and the sights, sounds and feeling of the place all blended together in my somnolent mind; I thought I had fallen into a chasm, a gash cut right through the globe of the earth; I felt myself being carried off without pain by a current of molten metal, and that a thousand such streams, whose color varied with their chemical composition, were coursing through the bowels of the earth like the blood vessels and veins which meander among the lobes of the brain. These streams were all flowing, circulating and pulsating in that fashion, and I had the feeling that they consisted of living souls, in a molecular state which only my speed of movement kept me from discerning. A whitish light gradually filtered into these conduits, and at last I saw open out, like a vast dome, a new horizon, on which I could make out islands lapped by luminous waves. Soon I found myself on a seacoast, in that same pallid, sunless daylight; and I saw an old man tilling the soil. I recognized him as the very person who had spoken to me through the voice of the bird; and it became clear to me, whether from what he was saying to me or by intuitive comprehension on my part, that our ancestors sometimes take the form of certain creatures to visit us on earth, and that in this way they are in attendance, as mute observers, at crucial stages of our existence.

The old man left his work and accompanied me to a house that stood near by. The surrounding country reminded me of a part of French Flanders where my forebears had lived and are now buried: the hedge-enclosed field adjoining the woodland, the lake not far away, the river and its washing-board, the village with its sloping street, the dark sandstone hills with their clumps of broom and heather—a rejuvenated image of the places I had loved. But the house I entered was not at all familiar to me. I understood that it had existed long before my time, and that in this world I was then visiting, the ghosts of material things accompanied that of the body.

I entered a large room where many people were gathered. Everywhere I looked there were familiar faces. The features of relatives whose deaths I had mourned were reproduced in other persons, dressed in old-fashioned clothes, who greeted me in the same familial fashion. They all seemed to have assembled for a family banquet. One of these relatives of mine came up and embraced me tenderly. He was wearing an old-fashioned costume whose colors looked faded, and his smiling face, under his powdered hair, bore some resemblance to my own. To me he seemed more vividly alive than the others, and somehow more naturally in tune with my mind and spirit. — This was my uncle. He made me sit next to him, and a kind of communication established itself between us; for I cannot say I heard his voice; but whenever my thoughts would be concentrated on a particular question, the answer thereto would at once become clear to me, and precise images would form before my eyes, like animated paintings.

"So it's true!" I said with delight. "We are immortal, and we retain here the images of the world we have lived in. What a joy, to think that everything we have loved will exist forever around us! . . . I was so very tired of life!"

"Do not rejoice too hastily," he said, "for you are still of the upper world, and have still some years of arduous testing to undergo. This abode which delights you so much has its own sorrows, its struggles and its dangers. The earth where we once lived is still the theater wherein the threads of our destiny are interwoven and unraveled; we are rays of that central fire which animates the earth, and which has already lost some of its strength . . ."

"What!" I exclaimed. "The earth might die, and leave us engulfed by nothingness?"

"Nothingness," he said, "does not exist in the way in which we think of it; but the earth is itself a material body, of which all spirits, collectively, are the soul. Matter cannot perish any more than can spirit, but it can be altered for good or evil. Our past and our future are interdependent. We live in our race, and our race lives in us."

This concept instantly became clearly perceptible to me; it was as if the walls of the room opened out upon limitless perspectives, and I seemed to see an unbroken chain of men and women in whom I existed and who existed in me; the costumes of all the peoples, the images of all the nations, appeared to me distinctly yet simultaneously, as if my faculties of attention had been multiplied without producing confusion—a spatial phenomenon analogous to the temporal one which can pack a century of action into a minute of dreaming. My astonishment was increased when I saw that all this vast enumeration comprised no more than

the persons then present in that room, whose images I had
seen divided and recombined in a thousand fleeting aspects.

"We are seven," I said to my uncle.

"That is indeed," he said, "the number typical of every
human family, and by extension, seven times seven, and so
on."*

I cannot hope to make the reader understand this reply,
which is still quite obscure even to me. Metaphysics pro-
vides me no term for the perception I then had of the
relationship between this number of persons and overall,
universal harmony. One can conceive, in the father and
mother, an analogy to nature's electrical forces; but what
can be said of the individual centers having emanated from
them, like a collective animistic *figure* or personality, capable of manifold combinations and at the same time subject
to mathematical restriction? One might just as well ask the
flower to account for the number of its petals or of divisions
in its corolla . . . the earth's surface for the number of
patterns it forms, or the sun for the number of colors it
produces.

ꝟ

Everything around me was changing form. The spirit
with whom I was conversing no longer looked the same. Now
he was a young man, and he was accepting ideas from me

---

* Seven was the number of Noah's family; but one of the seven belonged,
mysteriously, to the previous generations of the Elohim! . . .

. . . Imagination, like a bolt of lightning, presented to me the multiple
gods of India as images, so to speak, of the primally concentrated family.
I tremble to pursue this any further, for in the Trinity there resides yet
another awesome mystery . . . . We were born under Biblical law . . .

instead of enlightening me . . . Had I gone too far, up here in these dizzying heights? I seemed to sense that these were difficult or dangerous questions, even for the spirits inhabiting the world I was then perceiving. So perhaps a higher power was forbidding me to pursue this kind of research. I now found myself roaming the streets of a very populous city, unfamiliar to me. I noted that it was a city of hills, and that it was dominated by one high mountain entirely covered with habitations. Throughout the population of this capital city, I kept noticing particularly certain men who seemed to belong to a special nation; their vigorous, resolute air, the energetic cast of their features, made me think of the independent, warlike races of mountainous countries or of certain islands rarely visited by outsiders; yet it was here, in a great city and amidst a heterogeneous, communal population, that they were able to maintain in this fashion their fiercely individual character. Who or what were these men? My guide took me up some precipitous, bustling streets where the diverse sounds of industry could be heard. We climbed a long series of flights of steps to a vantage point where the view opened out before us. Here and there could be seen terraces enclosed by latticework; tiny, well-tended gardens in some level spots; rooftops and light, airy wooden pavilions painted and carved with whimsical patience. Whole vistas bound together by long trains of climbing greenery charmed the eye and soothed the spirit; it was like viewing a delightful oasis, a private, almost secret refuge where the noisy tumult of the city below was reduced to no more than a murmur. Much has been said about proscribed, outlaw nations, living in the shadows in necropolises and catacombs; here it was apparently just the opposite. A gifted race of people had created for themselves this haven, so happily shared by birds, flowers, pure air and sunlight. "They are," said my guide, "the original inhabitants of this mountain which dominates this city. For a long time they have lived their simple lives, loving and just, still retaining the natural virtues from the early days of creation. Their fellow-citizens hold them in high esteem and have tried to emulate them."

From where I was at that moment, I followed my guide down into one of those hillside dwellings whose collective roofs had such an unusual appearance. It seemed to me that my feet were sinking into successive layers of buildings of different ages. These phantom structures kept giving way to reveal others, in which could be distinguished the particular style and taste of each century; and this reminded me of the excavations made of ancient cities, except that everything was well-ventilated, teeming with life, and traversed by light in a thousand patterns. Finally I found myself in a huge room where I saw an old man sitting at a table, working at some sort of handcraft. The moment I crossed the threshold, a man dressed in white, whose features I could not make out clearly, threatened me with a weapon he held in his hand; but my companion motioned him aside. It was apparent that they would have preferred to keep me from penetrating the mystery of these retreats. Without asking any questions of my guide, I understood intuitively that these heights, as well as the underground spaces beneath them, had been the retreat of the aboriginal inhabitants of the mountain. In eternal defiance of the new races of people who, wave after wave, had continually invaded their home territory, they had gone right on living there; unsophisticated, loving and just, ingenious, skillful and tenacious, they had always conquered peacefully the ignorant hordes who had so many times usurped their heritage. Remarkable! Not corrupted, nor destroyed, nor enslaved; pure of heart, despite having conquered ignorance; conserving in prosperity all the virtues of poverty. — A child was amusing himself on the floor with some crystals, shells and carved stones, probably making a game out of a study assignment. An elderly but still beautiful woman was busying herself at household tasks. At that moment, several young men entered noisily, as if coming home from work. I was surprised to see them all dressed in white; but it seems this was an optical illusion on my part. To make me aware of this fact, my guide began to sketch their costumes; he tinted them with vivid colors, making me understand that this was how they really looked. The whiteness which had so surprised me was perhaps due to a special brilliance, an effect of light in which all the usual colors of the spectrum were fused into white. I left this room and went out onto a terrace arranged as a parterre, where some girls and young children were strolling about and playing. Their garments also looked white to me, although they were decorated with pink embroidery. These persons were so beautiful, their features so angelic, and the brightness of their souls showed so vividly through their delicate bodies that they all inspired in me a kind of undiscriminating love, free of desire, summing up the raptures of vague youthful passion.

I cannot express how it felt to be there among those charming beings who were dear to me without my being acquainted with them. They were like an original, heavenly family, their smiling eyes seeking mine with a tender compassion. I began to weep grievously, as if remembering a paradise lost. I sensed bitterly that I was only a transient in this strange yet beloved world, and I shuddered at the thought of having to leave it to return into life. In vain did the women and children press around me as if to keep me there. Already their delightful forms were dissolving into a vaporous haze; those beautiful faces were losing their color, and those strong features and sparkling eyes were disappearing into a dark shadow wherein the last bright flicker of their smiles continued to gleam.

Such was this vision, or such at least were the principal details of it which I remembered. The cataleptic state I had been in for several days was explained to me scientifically, and the accounts of those who had seen me in it caused me a kind of vexation, when I perceived that my actions or words, marking the different phases of what constituted for me a series of perfectly logical events, were being attributed to mental aberration. I was more favorably disposed toward those of my friends who, out of kindly tolerance or a personal predilection for ideas such as mine, encouraged me to give long, detailed account of the things I had seen as a spirit. One of them said to me, weeping: "There really is a God, isn't there?" "Yes!" I told him with enthusiasm. And we embraced, like long-lost brothers sharing that mystic homeland I had had a glimpse of. — What joy I found at first in my firm conviction! That everlasting doubt about the immortality of the soul which affects the best of minds was thereby resolved for me. No more death, no more sorrow, no more anxiety. The deceased relatives and friends I loved were giving me unmistakable signs of their eternal existence, and I was no longer separated from them except during the hours of daylight. I awaited those of night in a bittersweet melancholy.

VI

I had a dream which reinforced my confidence in this way of thinking. I suddenly found myself in a room of my grandfather's house. It seemed, however, to have been enlarged and beautified. The old furniture gleamed with a wonderful polish, the rugs and curtains were like new, a light three times as bright as natural daylight was coming

in through the casement-window and the door, and in the
air was the aromatic freshness of an early spring morning.
Three women were working in this room; and they represented, without absolutely resembling them, some female
relatives and friends of my youth. It seemed that each of the
three had the features of several such persons. The contours
of their faces kept changing shape, like the flame of a lamp,
and from moment to moment, some quality in one of them
would pass into another: smile, tone of voice, color of eyes,
color of hair, stature, habitual gestures—all was inter-
changeable, as though these women had all shared the same
life, so that each was a composite of the group, just as a
painter depicts a classic type from several models, in order
to achieve a perfect beauty.

The oldest one spoke to me in a vibrant, melodious voice
which I recognized from having heard it in childhood, and
something or other that she said to me impressed me
particularly with its profound rightness. But she drew my
attention to my own person, and I saw that I was dressed in
a little brown suit of old-fashioned cut, woven entirely by
hand with threads as tenuous as those of a spider's web. It
was stylish and graceful, and had a pleasing smell to it. I felt
very young and all spruced up to be wearing this garment
made by their magical, fairy hands, and I thanked them for
it, blushing as a small boy might in the presence of beautiful, grown-up ladies. Then one of them got up and moved
toward the garden.

Everyone knows that in dreams one never sees the sun,
although one often perceives a light of far greater brilliance.
Objects and bodies are luminous in themselves. I saw
myself in a small garden or yard with long, cradle-shaped
arbors laden with heavy bunches of white and black grapes;
as my lady guide moved along beneath these arbors, the
shadows of the intercrossing trellises seemed to me to be

making still more changes in her physical appearance and her clothing. At last she emerged from under the arbors, and we found ourselves in a spacious open area. Here there were barely discernible traces of two broad walkways which had once traversed it in the form of a cross. Cultivation of this area had been neglected for many years, and from scattered plantings of clematis, hops, honeysuckle, jasmine, ivy and birthwort came long trains of vigorously-growing vines, reaching from tree to tree. Branches loaded with fruit bent clear to the ground; and among thickets of weeds a few garden-flowers, having reverted to the wild state, were in bloom.

Spaced at intervals were groves of poplars, acacias and pines, within each of which one caught a glimpse of statuary blackened by the elements. I saw before me a heap of ivy-covered rocks from which gushed a fresh-water spring, its musical splash echoing across a stagnant pool half-hidden by the broad leaves of water-lilies.

The lady I was following, her slender figure moving in a way which made the folds of her taffeta dress shimmer with changing colors, gracefully cradled in her bare arm the tall stalk of a hollyhock; then, under a bright beam of light, she began to grow larger and larger, in such a way that the garden as a whole gradually assumed her shape, and the flower-beds and trees became the rosettes and scallops of her garments, while her face and arms imposed their contours on the purple clouds in the sky. As she became transfigured, I began to lose sight of her; she seemed to be vanishing into her own grandeur. "No, no—don't leave me!" I cried . . . "All nature is dying out with you!"

As I spoke these words, I struggled on painfully through the brambles, as if to grasp and hold that magnified, shadowy figure which was getting away from me; but I collided with a dilapidated segment of wall, at the foot of which lay the sculpted bust of a woman. Picking it up, I was persuaded at once that it was of *her* . . . I recognized certain beloved features, and upon looking around me, I saw that the garden had taken on the look of a cemetery. I heard voices saying: "The Universe is in darkness!"

VII

This dream, which had started out to be such a happy one, left me greatly perplexed. What did it mean? Not until later did I find out. Aurelia had died.

At first I heard only that she was very ill. Owing to my state of mind, I felt only a kind of vexation mingled with hope. I believed that I myself had only a short while to live, and for the future I was confident of our continuing to exist, in a world where loving hearts are reunited. Furthermore, she would belong to me in death much more than she did in life . . . A selfish thought, for which my reason was to pay later through bitter remorse.

I shouldn't want to make too much of premonitions; chance does strange things; but at that time I did vividly recall, and dwell upon, an incident of our too-brief union. I had given her a ring of antique workmanship, the setting of which was an opal shaped like a heart. This ring was too large for her finger, and I had had the unfortunate idea of having it cut, in order to reduce its circumference; not until I heard the sound of the saw did I realize my mistake. I seemed to see blood flowing . . .

Medical treatment had restored me to physical health without yet having got my mind back on the regular track of human reason. The house in which I found myself, situated on high ground, had behind it a large garden planted with fine trees. The pure air of that elevated site, the first breaths of spring and the pleasure of being with people I really liked brought me long hours of tranquility.

The first young leaves of the sycamores delighted me with the vivacity of their colors, like the plumes of Pharaoh's cocks. The view, which extended outward over the plain, presented, from morning till evening, pleasant horizons whose graduated hues stimulated my imagination. I peopled the hillsides and the clouds with divine figures whose shapes I seemed to see distinctly. — I resolved to fix my favorite thoughts more clearly in my mind, and with the aid of pieces of charcoal and brick I picked up, I soon covered the walls with a series of frescoes giving actual form to my impressions. One figure always dominated the rest: it was that of Aurelia, depicted with the features of a Deity, just as she had appeared in my dreams. Beneath her feet a wheel was turning, and the gods made up her retinue. I managed to color this group by using juices pressed from herbs and flowers. — How many times did I stand dreaming before that dear idol! I went still further; I tried to represent, with earth, the physical body of the one I loved. Every morning my work was all to be done over, for my fellow madmen, envious of my happiness, took pleasure in destroying my picture of it.

I was given some paper, and for a long time I applied myself to composing, with hundreds of drawings accompanied by narratives, verses and inscriptions in all the known languages, a sort of history of the world mixed with recollections of my student days and with fragments of dreams, which my obsession rendered more comprehensible or which prolonged its duration. I did not stop with the modern traditions concerning creation. My thinking went much farther back in time. I seemed to see, as if in memory, the original covenant made by the genii with their talismans. I tried to join together the stones of the *Sacred Table*, and to represent around it the seven[7] original *Elohim* who had divided the world among them.

This view of history, borrowed from Oriental traditions, began with the auspicious agreement among the Powers of Nature, who formulated and organized the universe. — During the night before I started this work, I had believed myself transported to a dark planet where the first seeds of creation were struggling into life. From the bosom of the still-soft clay rose gigantic palm-trees, poisonous spurges and acanthus vines twined around cacti; the shapes of stark, barren rocks rose like skeletons from this scene of incipient creation, and hideous reptiles slithered about, growing ever longer or thicker, inextricably tangled in wild, luxuriant vegetation. The bluish vistas and horizons of this strange world were illumined only by the pale light of the stars; but as fast as these new creations were formed, a single, brighter star would glean from them the seeds of light.

VIII

Then the monsters changed shape, and shedding their original skins, rose up more powerful than before on gigantic hind legs; the enormous weight of their bodies kept breaking tree-branches and undergrowth, and in the disor-

---

[7]Seven. A number of capital importance in the Bible, the Kabbalah, and the Pythagorean "law of numbers" which determines the materiality of the universe and the transmigration of souls. Bettina L. Knapp: ". . . the Sacred Seven Sky Generations."

der and confusion of nature they fought battles with each other in which I myself took part, for I too had a body as strange as theirs. Then all of a sudden there rang out in that lonely wilderness of ours a singular harmony, and it seemed that all the intermingled cries, roars and shrieks of the primitive beings were thenceforth modulated to that divine melody. As its notes succeeded one another in infinite variation, the planet's darkness was gradually dissipated, divine shapes appeared on the open greenswards and deep within the thick copses, and all the monsters I had seen, thenceforth tamed, cast off their queer shapes; some became men and women, while others were transformed into wild animals, fish and birds.

Who then had performed this miracle? One radiant Goddess controlled, in these new *avatars*, the rapid development of human beings. Then intra-racial distinctions were established, first within the order of birds, then among the animals, the fishes and the reptiles: these orders were the Divas, the Peris, the Undines and the Salamanders; every time one of these beings died, it would at once be reborn more beautiful in form, and would sing the praises of the gods. One of the Elohim, however, conceived the idea of creating a fifth race, composed of the elements of the earth, which was named the *Afrites*.[8] This was the signal for a total revolt among the Spirits, who refused to acknowledge these new possessors of the world. For untold thousands of years, there were conflicts which shed blood all over the globe. Three of the Elohim, with the Spirits of their races, were at last transported to the southern part of the earth, where they established vast kingdoms. They had carried off with

---

[8]*Afrites*. Henri Lemaitre: "In William Beckford's *Vathek* [1786], the Afrites are the palace guard of Eblis, the sovereign of Hell . . ."

them the secrets of the divine *cabala*[9] which binds the worlds together, and they derived their strength from worship of certain heavenly bodies, with which they still continued to communicate. These necromancers, banished to the ends of the earth, had conspired together to keep power in their own hands. Surrounded by women and slaves, each of these sovereigns had made sure that he could be reincarnated as one of his own sons. Their life span was one thousand years. When the time drew near for one of them to die, powerful members of the *cabala* would shut him up in a well-guarded sepulcher, where he would be fed elixirs and preservative substances. For a long time he would retain the appearance of life; then, like the chrysalis which spins its own cocoon, he would go to sleep for forty days, to be reborn in the body of an infant who would later be called to the throne of empire.

Meanwhile, the earth's life-giving powers were being exhausted by having to nourish these families, whose blood, without change, coursed through one scion after another. In vast underground vaults dug out beneath catacombs and under pyramids, they had amassed all the treasures of their ancestors and certain talismans to protect them against the anger of the gods.

It was in the center of Africa, beyond the Mountains of the Moon and ancient Ethiopia, that all these mysterious events took place: I myself suffered for a long time in captivity there, as did much of the human race. The dense thickets, once so green, now bore nothing but pale flowers and withered leaves; an implacable sun devoured and dev-

---

[9]The Kabbalah: a book of wisdom, of byzantine complexity, compiled by Jewish mystics in the Middle Ages, containing, among other things, interpretations of the hidden meanings in the Old Testament, some of them based on a theory of numbers and their signification.

astated the region, and the feeble descendants of the everlasting ruling dynasties seemed overwhelmed by the sheer
weight of being alive. That imposing, monotonous grandeur, regulated by hieratic etiquette and ceremony,
weighed heavily on all, without anyone's daring to break
away from it. The old rulers languished under the weight
of their crowns and imperial ornaments, surrounded by
physicians and priests whose knowledge assured them of
immortality. As for the people, locked forever into their
caste system, they had no prospect of long life or freedom.
Under barren, dying trees and at the mouths of dried-up
wells and springs, pale, emaciated children and young
women could be seen withering away on the dry grass. The
splendor of royal bedchambers, the majesty of colonnades,
the brilliance of raiment and adornment were small consolation for the perpetual hardships of life in these desolate
places.[10]

Soon populations were decimated by disease, animals
and plants died, and the immortals themselves were wast-
ing away beneath their stately garments. Suddenly a
scourge, greater than all the others, was visited upon the
earth to rejuvenate and save it. In the sky, Orion turned on
the water-cataracts; the spinning earth, top-heavy with ice
at the opposite pole, reversed its direction, and the seas,
spilling over their banks, poured in over the plateaus of
Africa and Asia; the floodwaters penetrated the sand and
filled the tombs and the pyramids, and for forty days a
mysterious ark sailed the seas, bearing the hope of a new
creation.

---

[10]A description much like this is to be found in Thomas De Quincey's *Confessions of an English Opium-Eater* (1821), with which Nerval was undoubtedly acquainted.

Three of the Elohim took refuge on the highest summit
of the African mountains. A bitter dispute arose among
them. Here my memory blurs, and I don't know the outcome
of that supreme conflict. But I can still see, standing on a
barren peak washed by the heaving waters, a woman with
disheveled hair, abandoned, weeping and crying out in her
struggle against death . . . Was she rescued? I do not know.
The gods, her brothers, had condemned her to die; but above
her head shone the Evening Star, pouring down its fiery
rays upon her brow.

The interrupted anthem of the earth and the heavens
once again rang out harmoniously, consecrating the accord
among the new races. And while the sons of Noah toiled and
sweated in the light of a new sun, the necromancers, hidden
away in their subterranean retreats, continued to keep
their precious secrets and lived on comfortably in silence
and darkness. From time to time they would emerge fur-
tively from their lairs to terrorize the living, or to dissemi-
nate among the wicked the baneful teachings of their occult
sciences.

Such were the memories I retraced, by a kind of intuition
of the past; with fearful, trembling hand I described and
depicted the hideous features of these accursed races. Everywhere the suffering image of the Eternal Mother kept
dying, weeping or languishing. As the dim civilizations of
Asia and Africa rose and fell, one saw repeated again and
again the same bloody scene of orgy and carnage which
those same spirits were continually reproducing, in varying
forms.[11]

The most recent such scene occurred at Granada, where

---

[11]Typical of some drug-induced experiences, particularly with LSD—
although in Nerval's case there is no question of drugs.

the sacred talisman gave way beneath the hostile blows of
the Christians and the Moors. How much longer will the
world have to suffer? — for the vengeful onslaughts of those
eternal enemies of ours are certain to be renewed under
other skies! They are the severed sections of the serpent
encircling the earth . . . Separated by the sword, the seg-
ments come back together in a hideous kiss, cemented by the
blood of mankind.

IX

Such were the images which appeared, one after another, before my eyes. Little by little my peace of mind was
restored, and at last I left that dwelling which was for me a
paradise. A long time afterward, certain fateful circumstances triggered a relapse, in which the interrupted series
of these strange visions was resumed. — I was walking out
in the country, deep in thought about a literary work dealing
with religious ideas. In passing by a certain house, I heard
a bird, speaking aloud a few words he had been taught to
say, and his apparent gibberish seemed to me to be making
sense; this reminded me of the vision recounted above, and
I shuddered, sensing that this was a bad omen. A few steps
farther on, I met a friend whom I had not seen for a long time
and who lived near by. He insisted on showing me around
his property, and in the course of that tour of inspection, he
had me climb up to an elevated terrace from which there was
a broad view of the horizon. The sun was just setting. In
descending a rustic staircase, I stumbled and fell, striking
my breast against the sharp corner of a piece of furniture. I
had enough strength to pick myself up and rush to the center
of the garden, thinking I had received a fatal blow but
wishing to have one last look at the sunset before I died.

Amid the regrets brought on by such a moment, I felt happy
to be dying this way, at this time of day, amidst trees, grape-
arbors and autumn flowers. But this turned out to be only a
fainting-spell, after which I still had strength enough to
regain my lodgings and put myself to bed. I became feverish;
I remembered where I had been when I fell, and recalled
that the fine view from that terrace had overlooked a
cemetery, the very one in which Aurelia's grave was situated. This really had not occurred to me until that moment;
were it not for that fact, I could have attributed my fall to the
shock such a sight would have given me. This in itself gave
me the idea of impending doom more clearly than ever, and
made me regret all the more that death had not come to
reunite me with her. Then, upon reflection, I told myself that
I was unworthy. Bitterly I pictured to myself the life I had
led since her death, reproaching myself not for having
forgotten her, which had certainly not occurred, but for
having insulted her memory by engaging in facile intrigues.
I thought of interrogating my slumber about all this, but *her*
image refused to appear any more in my dreams as it had so
often done before. At first I had only confused dreams filled
with scenes of bloodshed. It seemed as if a whole new race
of sinister, deadly beings had been turned loose in the midst
of that ideal world I had seen before, and of which she was
the Queen. The same Spirit who had threatened me when I
entered the dwellings of those simple, honest families living
high up in the *Mysterious City* passed me by, no longer in the
white costume he had worn before, like the others of his race,
but in the garb of an Oriental prince. I sprang after him
threateningly, but he calmly turned round to face me. O
terror! O rage! It was my own face, my own body, idealized
and enlarged . . . Then I remembered that fellow who had
been arrested the same night I was, and who I thought had
been released from the guard-house under my name, when

my two friends had come to get me. He held in his hand a weapon, the shape of which I could not make out clearly; and one of the persons accompanying him said: "That's what he struck him with."

I cannot explain the fact that, in my thoughts, terrestrial events could and did coincide with those of the supernatural world; this is easier to *sense* than to enunciate clearly. But just who was this spirit who was myself and yet outside of me? Was he the *Double* of the legends, or the mysterious brother the Orientals call *Ferouër*?[12] — Had I not perhaps been excessively impressed by the story of the knight who spent all night fighting in a forest against a stranger, who turned out to be himself? Be that as it may, it is my belief that the human imagination has never invented anything that does not really exist, either in this world or in another; and I could not doubt the reality of what I had so distinctly *seen*.

A terrible idea struck me: "Man is dual," I said to myself. — "I feel two men within myself," wrote a certain Father of the Church. The coming together of two souls has deposited its composite seed inside a body, whose duality of origin is visibly evident in every organic element of its structure. In each man there is a spectator and an actor, a speaker and a responder. The Orientals have seen in this two enemies: the good and the evil genius. "Am I the good one? Or am I the evil one?" I asked myself. "In either case, the *other one* is hostile

---

[12]*Ferouër*. In Nerval's *Voyage en Orient*, the Calif Hakem saw his *"ferouër*, or his double, and . . . to see one's own specter is a sign of the worst augury." Henri Lemaitre: "Reappearance of the *double* . . . but this time with the idealization that takes its point of departure from the sonnet 'El Desdichado,' wherein the poet is, as here, *widower* and prince." Cf. Euripides' *Helen*, Kleist's *Amphitryon*, Gogol's "The Nose" and Dostoevsky's early story "The Double."

to me ... Who knows whether, under certain circumstances or at a certain age, these two spirits separate from each other? Both of them being bound by a material affinity to the same body, perhaps the one is destined for glory and happiness, the other for annihilation or eternal torment?" Suddenly this obscurity was traversed by a fatal flash of lightning ... Aurelia was no longer mine! I seemed to hear people talking about a ceremony that was in progress somewhere else, and about the preparations for a mystic wedding—my own—in which the *other one*, taking advantage of my friends' mistake, was going to get Aurelia. The persons most dear to me who kept coming to see and console me seemed to be a prey to uncertainty and ambivalence; that is to say, the two parts of their souls were divided where I was concerned—one part affectionate and trusting, the other mortally antagonistic toward me. There was a double meaning to everything these persons said to me, although they may not have been aware of this, since they were not *in spirit* as I was. At one moment, this idea struck me as comical: I thought of Amphitryon[13] and Sosia.[14] But what if this grotesque symbolism was something else—what if, as in other fables of antiquity, it was the fatal truth beneath a mask of madness? "All right," I said to myself, "let's do battle

---

[13]Amphitryon: a Theban prince, husband to Alcmena. Zeus assumed the form of Amphitryon while the real Amphitryon had gone off to war; the child Zeus sired by Alcmena was Hercules. In additon to Heinrich von Kleist (see note 12), Plautus, Molière, Dryden and Giraudoux have written dramas based on this legend.

[14]Sosia: Amphitryon's male slave. The god Mercury takes on the form of Sosia, on the orders of Jupiter (Zeus), to prevent the real Sosia from reaching Alcmena with a message from the real Amphitryon. Nerval's source is undoubtedly Molière.

with the fatal spirit; let's take on the god himself, with tradition and knowledge as our weapons. Whatever he may do out there in the dark, I do exist; and I have at my disposal, to defeat him, all the time still left to me to live on earth."

X

How to describe the strange state of despair to which these thoughts gradually reduced me? An evil genius had usurped my place in the world of souls; for Aurelia, that spirit was I myself, and the forlorn spirit which still animated my body, enfeebled, scorned, unrecognized by her, was forever doomed to despair and oblivion. I brought all my will-power to bear, in an effort to penetrate further the mystery from which I had lifted some of the veils. My dreams sometimes made a mockery of my efforts by bringing into my head nothing but ephemeral, grimacing faces. I can offer here only a rather bizarre notion of what this mental intensity of mine brought about. I felt myself sliding as if on a wire of infinite length. The earth, traversed as I had observed before by colored veins of molten metals, was gradually growing brighter from the overflowing of its central fire, whose whiteness was blending into the cherry-red hues coloring the sides of its inner core. From time to time I was surprised to encounter huge puddles of water suspended in the air like clouds, but of such density that pieces could be detached from them; this was obviously a liquid quite different from terrestrial water, no doubt the evaporation from whatever constituted the seas and rivers of the spirit world.

I arrived within view of a vast beach, hilly and overgrown with a kind of reeds, greenish in color, but yellowed at the tips as if the heat of the sun had partially withered them, —but I saw no more of the sun than I had on previous occasions. — I began to climb one of the hills, which had a castle on top of it. Beyond this hill I saw a great city spreading out before me. Night had fallen while I was climbing, and I could see lights in the houses and streets. Upon coming down into the city, I found myself in a market where fruits and vegetables like those of the Midi were being offered for sale.

I descended a dark stairway and found myself in the streets. Posters were being put up, advertising the opening of a casino and describing in detail the prizes being offered. The printed framing of the posters consisted of garlands of flowers, so well-drawn and -colored that they looked real. One building was still under construction. I entered a workshop where I saw something shaped like a llama, but apparently to be equipped with large wings. This monster was somehow being injected with a jet of fire which was gradually bringing it to life, so that it writhed about, penetrated by hundreds of crimson networks to form arteries and veins fecundating, as it were, the inert matter; its exterior was being covered instantaneously by a full growth of fibrous appendages, pinions and tufts of woolly hair. I stopped to contemplate this masterpiece, in which the secrets of divine creation seemed to have been revealed. "The fact is that we have here," I was told, "the primal fire which first ignited life in created beings . . . Long ago, it leaped up to the surface of the earth; but its sources have dried up." I saw also some pieces of jewelry in which two metals unknown on earth were used: one red, which seemed to be something like cinnabar, and the other sky-blue. These ornaments had been neither hammered nor chiseled, but had acquired their form and color simply by "blooming," like the metallic vegetation produced by the interreaction of certain chemicals. "Couldn't one create men also?" I asked one of the workmen; but he replied: "Men come from above, not from below; can we create ourselves? All we are doing here is formulating, thanks to successive advances in our industrial technology, some new substances more subtle than any of those composing the earth's crust. These flowers which look so natural to you, this animal which may seem to be alive, are merely products of our technical skill, based on highly-developed scientific knowledge; and everyone should judge them as such."

This is approximately what I learned, either in the very words spoken to me, or in words whose meaning I believed I had correctly understood. I started to walk through the rooms of the casino, and there I saw a large crowd of people, among whom I discovered persons of my acquaintance, some of them living, others who had died at various times in the past. The former appeared not to see me, while the latter returned my greeting without seeming to know who I was. Soon I found myself in the great hall, which was all draped in poppy-red velvet with rich designs woven into it in cloth of gold. In the center of the hall stood an upholstered settee in the form of a throne. Passers-by were sitting down on it for a moment to test its elasticity; but since all was not yet in readiness, they kept moving off to other rooms. There was talk of a wedding and of the groom, who they said was supposed to arrive soon to signal the beginning of the festivities. I imagined that he who was being awaited was my *double*, who was going to be married to Aurelia; and I made a scene which seemed to dismay the assembly. I began talking violently, expounding my grievances and invoking the assistance of all those present who knew me. One old man said to me: "But one just doesn't behave this way; you're frightening everybody." Whereupon I shouted: "I know well enough that he has already struck me with his weapons; but

I'm not afraid of him, and I know the sign that will defeat him."

At that moment one of the workmen from the workshop I had visited came in, holding a long metal rod, the end of which was a red-hot, round ball. I attempted to rush him, but he continued to hold the ball in a parrying position, threatening my face. People around me seemed to be taunting me for my impotence . . . Then I retreated as far as the throne, my soul full of ineffable pride, and raised my arm to make a certain sign which seemed to me to possess magical power. The cry of a woman, distinct and resonant, awoke me with a start! The syllables of an unknown word I was about to pronounce expired on my lips . . . I dropped quickly to my knees on the floor and began to pray furiously, weeping bitterly. — But what was it, that voice which had just rung out so distressfully in the darkness?

It was not a part of the dream; it was the voice of a living person, and yet for me it was the voice of Aurelia . . .

I opened my window; all was quiet, and the cry was not repeated. — When I made inquiries outside, no one had heard anything. — And yet I am still certain that the cry was real, that it had echoed in the air of the living world . . . There will be those who say, no doubt, that some woman in the neighborhood of my lodgings really did happen to cry out in grief or pain at that precise moment. — But it is my firm belief that terrestrial events were synchronized with events in the invisible world. This is one of those strange linkages which I myself do not understand, and which are easier to observe than to explain.

What had I done? I had disturbed the harmony of that magical universe wherein my soul had sought and found certain assurance of immortal existence. I was damned, perhaps, for having attempted, in violation of divine law, to probe into a forbidden mystery; henceforth I might expect nothing but wrath and contempt! The spirits, vexed, were flying away, uttering cries and tracing ominous circles in the air, like birds at the approach of a storm.

PART TWO

Eurydice!   Eurydice!

I

Lost, a second time!

All is over, all is ended! Now it's my turn to die, and to die without hope. — What then is death? Suppose it is mere oblivion . . . Would to God it were! But God himself cannot make death be nothing but oblivion.

Now why was this the first time I had thought of Him in such a long while? In the fatal cosmic system which had taken shape within my mind, there was no place for that solitary Majesty . . . or rather He was absorbed into the sum of all beings; He was the god of Lucretius,[15] powerless and lost in His own immensity.

She, however, had believed in God; and one day I had caught the name of Jesus on her lips, a sound so sweet that I had wept to hear it. Dear God! Those tears . . . they have

---

[15]Titus Lucretius Carus (ca. 99-55 B.C.). In a letter to Gaius Memmius he states: "The world had a beginning and will have an end; it was not created by the gods, who are remote and unconcerned." Legend has it that a love potion given him by his wife drove him mad, causing his suicide.

been dried so long! Dear God! Please give them back to me!

When the soul is floating in limbo between real life and dreams, between mental chaos and the return of cold reflection, it is to religious thought that one must turn for succor;—I have never been able to find solace in philosophy, which offers us nothing but maxims of egoism or at best reciprocity, vain experience, and bitter doubts; it combats mental and spiritual pain by annihilating sensibility; like surgery, all it can do is to cut out a part of the pain-causing organ. — But for us, born in a time of revolution and upheaval, in which all faiths and beliefs have been shattered, — brought up at best in that kind of "faith" which demands no more than external observance of certain practices, and to which indifferent adherence is perhaps more culpable than godlessness or heresy—it is very difficult, once we feel the need of it, to reconstruct the mystic edifice whose fully-delineated form is wholeheartedly and unquestioningly accepted by naïve, simple people. "The tree of knowledge is not the tree of life!" But can we dismiss entirely from our collective mind what intelligent persons of so many generations have contributed to it, right or wrong, good or evil? Ignorance cannot teach us anything.

I have higher hopes for the goodness of God: perhaps we are approaching the predicted era when science, having completed its entire cycle of analysis and synthesis, of belief and denial, will rise to new heights of purity to build, out of chaos and ruin, the marvelous city of the future . . . One must not hold human reason so cheaply as to think it will gain anything by humbling itself completely, for to do so would be to impugn its celestial origin . . . Surely God will appreciate purity of intentions—and what father would be pleased to see his son renounce, in his presence, all common sense and self-respect? The disciple who wanted to touch in order to believe was not condemned for that!

* * *

What is all this that I have written here? It is blas-
phemy. Christian humility cannot speak so. Thoughts like
these are far from soul-soothing. They wear on their brow
the crown of Satan, the lightning-bolts of pride . . . A pact
with God Himself? O science, O vanity!

* * *

I had collected a number of books on Cabala.[16] Immers-
ing myself in this occult study, I came to the conclusion that
it was all true, everything the human mind had accumu-
lated on this subject over the centuries. My already-formed
conviction of the existence of the outer world coincided too
well with my readings to leave me in any doubt about the
truth of past revelations. The dogmas and rites of the
various religions all appeared to me to relate to those
revelations in such a way that each religion possessed
certain elements of the great mystery, elements which
constituted its means of expansion and defense. When at
times these powers became enfeebled, dwindled and disappeared, this led to the conquest of certain races by others,
not one of them ever conquering or being conquered except
by the power of the spirit.

"Still," I said to myself, "it is certain that these sciences
are replete with human error. The magic alphabet, the
mysterious hieroglyph, reach us only in a defective, corrupted form, altered and falsified either by time or by those
beings who have a vested interest in our remaining ignorant; if only we can identify the missing letter or the

---

[16]See note 9 on the Kabbalah.

obliterated sign, if we can resolve the dissonance of the scale, we shall learn a great deal about the spirit world."

This was how I perceived the connection between the real world and the spirit world: The earth, together with its inhabitants and their history, is the theater wherein take place the physical actions which prepare for the existence and determine the situation of immortal beings attached to its destiny. Without addressing the impenetrable mystery of the eternity of the universe, my thoughts went back to the time when the sun, like its namesake flower which follows with bowed head its orbital path across the heavens, sowed the earth with fertile seeds of plants and animals. This was nothing more nor less than fire itself, which, being compounded of souls, formulated instinctively their common dwelling-place. The spirit of the God-Being, reproduced and, as it were, reflected on the earth, became the prototype of certain human souls, each of whom, as a result, was at once both man and God. These were the Elohim.

* * *

When one is feeling wretched, he thinks about the misfortunes of others. I had been remiss in failing to visit one of my dearest friends, who I had been told was ill. As I drew near the place where he was being treated, I reproached myself bitterly for this delinquency. I was even more devastated when my friend told me later that he had been at the point of death the night before. I entered a sunny, whitewashed hospital room. Sunlight was tracing cheerful angular patterns on the walls and playing over a vase of flowers which a nun had just placed on the patient's table. This was almost the cell of an Italian anchorite. My friend's emaciated countenance, his yellowed-ivory complexion accentuated by the blackness of his beard and hair, his eyes still glittering with a touch of fever, perhaps also the effect of a hooded mantle thrown over his shoulders, made him seem to me a person very different from the one I had always known. No longer was he the merry companion of my work and pleasure; there was something of the apostle about him. He related to me how during the night, his malady having reached its most painful crisis, he had been seized by one climactic spasm which he was sure would be the end of him. All at once, as if by a miracle, the pain had ceased. — It's impossible for me to render accurately his account of what happened thereafter: a sublime dream of finding himself in the outermost reaches of the infinite, of speaking with another being, — himself, yet not himself, — whom he had asked, believing himself to be dead, where God was. "Why, God is everywhere," replied his spirit. "He is within yourself and within everyone. He judges you, listens to you, counsels you; he is you *and I*, who think and dream as one—and we have never been apart, and we are eternal!"

I cannot quote anything else from that conversation, which I may not have heard or understood correctly. I know only that it made a very strong impression upon me. I dare not attribute to my friend the conclusions I drew, perhaps mistakenly, from his words. I cannot even be sure whether their import is, or is not, consonant with Christian doctrine.

"God is with him," I cried, "but He is no longer with me! O catastrophe! I have driven Him away from me; I threatened Him, cursed Him! It was He all right, within that mystic brother of mine, getting farther and farther away from my soul, and warning me, in vain! That preferred bridegroom, that king of glory, — it is He who now judges and condemns me, and who is carrying off forever to His heaven the woman whom He might have given to me, and of whom I am henceforth unworthy!"

II

I cannot describe the state of despondency these thoughts cast me into. "I understand," I said to myself. "I have preferred the created being over the Creator; I have deified my love and have worshiped, pagan-fashion, a woman whose last mortal sigh was of self-dedication to Christ. But if this religion speaks true, God may yet pardon me. He may give her back to me if I humble myself before Him; perhaps her spirit will return, within me!" I roamed the streets at random, full of this idea. I encountered a funeral procession; it was bound for the cemetery where she had been buried; I resolved to join it and go there also. "I don't know," I said to myself, "who this dead man is who is being borne to his grave; but I do know that the dead see us and hear us, —perhaps he will be pleased to see himself followed by someone more grief-stricken than any of the mourners accompanying him." This idea caused me to shed tears, and people undoubtedly thought I was a close friend of the deceased. O blessed tears! Your sweetness has been denied me for so long! . . . My head cleared, and a ray of hope still led me on. I felt strong enough to pray, and did so with rapture.

I did not even inquire who it was whose coffin I had followed. The cemetery I had entered was sacred to me on several counts. Three members of my mother's family had been buried there; but I could not go to their graves to pray, for they had been removed several years before to a distant land, their place of origin. — I looked for a long time for Aurelia's grave, but could not find it. The layout of the cemetery had been changed, —or perhaps my memory had failed me . . . It seemed to me that this incident, this forgetfulness, was heaping still more condemnation upon me. I dared not mention to the caretakers the name of a dead

woman to whom I had no ties sanctioned by religion . . . But
I recalled that I had at home a paper showing the exact
location of her grave, and I ran home to get it, my heart
pounding and my head in a whirl. As I have already said, I
had built up around this love of mine some bizarre superstitions. In a small box which had belonged to *her*, I had kept
her last letter. In fact, I must confess that I had made of this
box a sort of reliquary, keeping in it souvenirs from long
trips during which thoughts of her had been always with me:
a rose picked in the gardens of Schoubrah, a piece of
mummy-wrapping brought back from Egypt, some laurel
leaves gathered along the river Beyrouth, two gilded-glass
miniatures of the mosaics of St. Sophia, a rosary bead, some
other things . . . and finally, the piece of paper I had been
given, the day her grave was being dug, to help me locate it.
I blushed, I shuddered as I spread this crazy collection out
before me. I put the two papers into my pocket, and then,
just as I was about to start back to the cemetery, I changed
my mind. "No," I said to myself. "I am not worthy to kneel at
the grave of a Christian woman; let's not add still another
profanation to so many! . . ." And to calm the storm that was
raging inside my head, I left Paris and went to a small town
a few miles away where as a youth I had spent many happy
hours at the home of some elderly relatives of mine, since
deceased. I had enjoyed coming there often to watch the sun
go down from a vantage point near their house. There was
also a terrace there, shaded by linden-trees, which reminded me of some girl cousins I had grown up with. One of
them . . .

But could I really have been thinking of comparing that
kind of childish puppy-love to the love that had devoured my
youth? I watched the sun sink slowly over the valley, which
gradually filled with mist and shadows; at last the sun
disappeared, bathing in a reddish glow the tree-tops on the

ridge of the high hills. The gloomiest melancholy filled my heart. I took a room for the night at an inn where I was known. The innkeeper told me about an old friend of mine, a local resident, who as a consequence of some unfortunate speculation had killed himself with a pistol . . . That night, sleep brought me some terrible dreams, of which I have only a hazy recollection. — I was in an unfamiliar room, talking with someone from the other world, —perhaps the old friend just mentioned. Behind me stood a very tall mirror. Happening to glance at it, I seemed to see Aurelia. She looked sad and pensive, and all of a sudden—whether she emerged from the mirror, or whether she had been reflected in it a moment before as she came into the room—that sweet, dear figure was there beside me. She held out her hand to me, gave me a sorrowful look and said: "We shall meet again later . . . at your friend's house."

Thinking instantly of her marriage, of the curse that kept us apart . . . I said to myself: "Is it possible? Could she be coming back to me?" With tears in my eyes, I asked: "Have you forgiven me?" But all had disappeared. I found myself in a lonely, uninhabited place, on a steep, rock-strewn hill surrounded by forests. Standing high above this desolate country was a house, which I seemed to recognize. I kept going back and forth, this way and that, trying to find my way through an inextricable maze of detours. Tired of walking through stones and brambles, I kept looking for an easier route via footpaths through the woods. I kept thinking: "They're waiting for me over there!" — A certain hour struck . . . I said to myself: "*It's too late!*" Voices replied: "*She is lost!*" All around me was utter darkness; but the house in the distance shone brightly, as if lighted for a party and already filled with punctual guests. "She is lost!" I cried to myself. "And why? I understand—she made a final effort to save me; —and I missed the crucial moment when a pardon was still possible. Up there in heaven, she was able to beseech the Divine Bridegroom on my behalf . . . But what does it matter—even my very salvation? The abyss has claimed its victim! She is lost, to me and to everyone! . . ." And I seemed to see her as if by the light of a lightning flash, pale and dying, being carried off by dark horsemen . . . The cry of grief and rage I uttered at that moment woke me up, gasping for breath. "O God, dear God! For her sake, for her sake alone, dear God, Thy pardon!" I cried, falling to my knees.

It was daylight. Acting in a way I find difficult to account for, I resolved to destroy then and there the two papers I had taken out of the box the night before: the letter, which— alas!—I read once more, soaking it with tears, and the melancholy document bearing the seal of the cemetery. "Find her grave now?" I said to myself. "It was yesterday that I should have gone back there—and my fatal dream is only a portent of my doomsday!"

III

The flames devoured those two relics of love and death, so tightly entwined with my heartstrings. I took my troubles and my belated remorse for a long walk out in the country, seeking by physical exertion and fatigue to dull my thinking and perhaps assure myself some less troubled sleep the following night. Because of that idea I had conceived, that dreams are an avenue of communication between man and the spirit world, I hoped . . . I still hoped! Perhaps God would be content with this sacrifice. — Here I must stop; it would be too prideful of me to claim that my state of mind had been brought about solely by a lost love remembered. Let us rather say that I was involuntarily using the latter to embellish my truly grave remorse for a foolishly wasted life, in which evil had very often triumphed, and whose misdeeds I had never acknowledged until calamity struck me. I no longer considered myself worthy even to *think* about that person whom I had been harassing in death after having caused her so much pain in life, and to whose sweet, saintly pity alone I owed the final look of forgiveness she had given me.

The following night I was able to sleep only fitfully. A woman who had taken care of me when I was a boy appeared to me in a dream and reproached me for a very grave offense I had committed long ago. I recognized her, although she looked much older than when I had last seen her. That very fact made me recall and regret bitterly that I had failed to go to see her when she lay dying. She seemed to be saying to me: "You did not weep as bitterly for your old relatives as for that woman. How can you expect forgiveness?" Then the dream became indistinct. The faces of some people I had known at different periods of my life passed rapidly before my eyes. They appeared one by one, becoming clear, fading, and falling away into darkness, like beads flying off the broken string of a rosary. Then I saw vaguely taking shape some sculpted figures from antiquity, roughly formed at first, then becoming clearly defined; they seemed to constitute a kind of symbolism, whose import was difficult for me to grasp; but I had the feeling that they meant: "All this has been done to teach you the secret of life, and you have failed to understand. Religions and fables, saints and poets have joined forces to make the great enigma clear to you, and still you have interpreted it wrongly. And now it's too late!"

I awoke utterly terrified, saying to myself as I arose: "This is my last day!" After an interval of ten years, the same obsession which I described in Part One of this narrative was coming back upon me, more absolute and more menacing than ever. God had allowed me this much time in which to repent, and I had put it to no use whatsoever. After the visit of the *stone guest*,[17] I had sat down again to the feast!

IV

The mental depression resulting from these visions, and from the reflections they inspired whenever I was alone, was so severe that I felt I was doomed. All the actions of my lifetime passed in review before me, every deed appearing in its most unfavorable light; and in the kind of moral examination to which I subjected myself, I recalled with singular clarity every single thing I had ever done, no matter how long ago. Some sort of reticence or embarrassment kept me from presenting myself at the confessional; perhaps it was the fear of getting involved in the dogmas and practices of a formidable religion, certain aspects of which I was still philosophically prejudiced against. My early years had been too thoroughly impregnated with the ideas spawned by the Revolution; I had been reared in too much freedom, had seen too much of the world, to accept easily a yoke which in many respects would still have insulted my intelligence. I shudder to think what kind of Christian I might have become, if certain principles derived from independent study of the history of the past two centuries, as well as from the study of various religions, had

---

[17]*Stone guest*. Don Juan killed the Commander in a duel over the latter's daughter; the statue on the Commander's tomb is jokingly invited by Don Juan to a banquet, and arrives there to drag the famous lover into hell. Tirso de Molina (1571-1641) penned the earliest Don Juan play; later versions of the legend are by Molière, Shadwell, Byron, Grabbe, Browning, Shaw and many others. Greatest of all is Mozart's opera *Don Giovanni* (1787) to a racy libretto by Lorenzo da Ponte.

not stopped me from drifting in that direction. I never knew my mother, who had tried to follow my father to the wars, like the women of the ancient Germanic peoples; she died of fever and exhaustion in a cold region of Germany, and my father himself failed to give me any early guidance in these matters. The region where I was brought up was full of legends and superstitions. An uncle of mine, the person who had the greatest influence on my early education, collected Roman and Celtic antiquities as a hobby. From time to time he used to find, in his own field or its vicinity, likenesses of gods and emperors; his scholarly admiration for them caused me to venerate them, and I learned their history from his books. A certain Mars in gilded bronze, an armed Pallas or Venus, a sculpted Neptune and Amphitrite over the village fountain, and especially a fine, fat, bearded figure of the god Pan smiling at the entrance to a grotto, among festoons of birthwort and ivy, were the domestic and tutelary gods of this retreat. I confess that they inspired in me, at that time, more veneration than did the poor Christian images in our church and the two misshapen saints on its portal, whom certain scholars have claimed to be the Gauls' Esus and Cernunnos. Confused amid all these diverse symbols, I asked my uncle one day what God was. "God is the sun," he told me. This was the deep-seated conviction of a good man who had been a Christian all his life, but who had lived through the Revolution, and who came from a region where many other people shared that same conception of the Deity. This did not prevent the women and children from attending church, and I owed to an aunt of mine some formal instruction which made me aware of the beauty and grandeur of Christianity. After 1815, an Englishman who happened to be in our area taught me the Sermon on the Mount and gave me a New Testament.... I cite these details merely to show why, in my mind and character, a certain hesitancy about religion has often coexisted with a profoundly religious spirit.

I want to make clear how, after straying so far from the true path for so long, I have felt myself brought back to it by the cherished memory of a deceased person, and how the need to believe that she still exists has brought home to my mind and heart a precise appreciation of certain verities which I had not embraced firmly enough within my soul. For anyone who lacks faith in immortality, in its punishments and rewards, certain stressful situations may result in despair and suicide; — I believe I shall have done something good, something helpful to others, by setting forth candidly, in their natural progression, the concepts and ideas through which I have found peace and a new strength to cope with life's future calamities.

The visions which had appeared to me one after another during sleep had reduced me to such despair that I could hardly talk; the company of my friends meant nothing to me but a kind of distraction; my mind, totally preoccupied by these illusions, was closed to any idea unrelated to them. Inwardly I kept making excuses for myself: "What's the difference? That doesn't exist for me." One of my friends, Georges by name,[18] undertook to overcome my despondency. He took me on short trips to various places on the outskirts of Paris, and willingly did all the talking himself, while I spoke only a few disjointed phrases in reply. One day, his expressive, almost cenobitic face lent great effect to some very eloquent things he found to say in deprecation of those years of skepticism and of political and social depression

---

[18]Georges Bell (1824-1899), born Joachim Hounau. Nerval's first biographer, called by Henri Lemaitre "one of the best friends of Gérard's last years."

which had followed the July Revolution. I had been of the younger generation during that period, and had tasted of its ardors and its rancors. Something within me stirred; I said to myself that lessons such as this one could not be given unless Providence willed it so, and that there was undoubtedly a spirit speaking to me through Georges... One day we were having dinner under an arbor in a little village on the outer edge of Paris; a woman came near our table and sang for us, and there was something about her tired but pleasing voice which reminded me of Aurelia's. I looked closely at her: even her facial features were not without some resemblance to those I had so loved. She was told to go away, and I dared not detain her, but I said to myself: "Who knows, perhaps *her spirit* is within that woman!" And I felt glad that I had given her some money.

I said to myself: "I have misused my life very badly; but if the dead do forgive us, it is undoubtedly on condition that we abstain henceforth from doing evil, and that we make amends for all the evil we have done. Is this possible?... From this moment on, let us try to do evil no more, and let us pay all our debts in full, whatever they may be." There was a certain person whom I had recently offended. The offense was due to mere negligence, but I began by going to him and apologizing for it. The joy this act of reparation gave me did me a great deal of good; from then on, I had a reason for living and acting; I was taking an interest once again in the world around me.

But difficulties arose: some events I found inexplicable seemed to conspire to thwart my good resolution. The condition of my mind made it impossible for me to accomplish the jobs I had contracted for. Thinking I was now in good health, people became more demanding; and since I had renounced all deception, I kept finding myself being taken advantage of by persons who had no such compunction. The mass of reparations to be made overwhelmed me because of my incapacity. Political events affected me indirectly, both by distressing me mentally and by depriving me of the means to put my affairs in order. Then to top off all these reasons for discouragement, a friend of mine died. I saw again with sorrow his house and his paintings, which he had shown me with great pleasure only a month before; I walked past his coffin at the moment when it was being nailed shut. As he was of my own age group, I said to myself: "What would happen if I were to die suddenly like that?"

The following Sunday, I got up feeling overwhelmed with grief and depression. I went to see my father, whose servant was ill and who seemed to be in a bad humor. He insisted on going alone to his storehouse for some wood, and the only service I was allowed to render him was to hand him a log he needed. I left in dismay. On the street I met a friend who asked me to go home with him for dinner, hoping to distract me a bit. I declined, and without having eaten anything, headed for Montmartre. The cemetery was closed, which I regarded as a bad omen. A German poet[19] had given me several pages to translate, paying me a sum in advance. I set out for his house, to return the money to him.

As I rounded the Clichy barrier, I found myself witness to a fight. I tried to separate the combatants, but failed. At that moment, a tall workman passed by, walking over the very spot where the fight had just taken place, carrying on his left shoulder a small child in a hyacinth-colored dress. I imagined that he was Saint Christopher carrying the Christ-child, and that I was being condemned for having displayed weakness in the incident that had just occurred. then I began wandering about, a prey to desperation, in the

---

[19]Heinrich Heine (1797-1856).

vacant lots which separate the faubourg from the barrier. When it was too late to make the visit I had planned, I started back through the streets toward the center of Paris. Somewhere on the Rue de la Victoire, I met a priest, and in my confused state of mind, tried to make confession to him. He told me that this was not his parish and that he was on his way to spend the evening at someone's house; that if I wished to consult him the next day at Notre-Dame, I had only to ask for Abbé Dubois.

Desperate and weeping, I headed for Notre-Dame de Lorette, where I prostrated myself at the foot of the altar of the Virgin, asking forgiveness for my transgressions. Something inside me said: "The Virgin is dead, and your prayers are useless." I went and knelt in the last row of the chancel, and I slipped off my finger a silver ring on whose setting were engraved, in Arabic, three words: "Allah! Mohammed! Ali!" Directly some candles were lighted in the chancel, and a service was begun, in which I made an effort to participate mentally. During the *Ave Maria*, the priest who was officiating paused momentarily and then resumed speaking, seven times in all, without my ever being able to remember what words were to come next. After completing the orison, the priest made some remarks which seemed to me to be intended for me alone. When the service was over and the candles were extinguished, I stood up, left the church and headed for the Champs-Elysées.

By the time I reached the Place de la Concorde, I was thinking of destroying myself. Several times I started toward the Seine, but something prevented me from carrying out my intention. The stars were shining brilliantly in the firmament. Suddenly I had the impression that all of them had just gone out, all at once, like the candles I had seen in the church. I thought our time had come—that we were about to witness the end of the world, as predicted in the

Apocalypse of Saint John. I thought I saw a black sun[20]in the empty sky and a blood-red globe hanging over the Tuileries. I said to myself: "The eternal night is beginning, and it is going to be frightful. What will happen when men realize that there is no sun any more?" I came back along the Rue Saint-Honoré, feeling pity for the belated peasants I kept meeting. I walked on as far as the Place du Louvre, and there a strange spectacle awaited me. Through clouds being driven rapidly before the wind, I sighted several moons passing overhead at great speed.[21] I thought that the earth had left its orbit and was wandering about the firmament like a dismasted ship, coming closer to the stars or veering away from them, making them appear larger or smaller by turns. For two or three hours I sat contemplating all this confusion, and finally I started off in the direction of the city market. The peasants were bringing in their produce, and I thought: "How amazed they will be when they see that the dark of night is being prolonged . . ." But I did hear dogs barking here and there, and cocks crowing.

Tired out, I went home and threw myself on my bed. Upon awakening, I was surprised to see light again. A kind of mysterious choir-music fell on my ear: childish voices were repeating in chorus: *Christe! Christe! Christe!* I thought a large number of children had been assembled in the neighboring church (Notre-Dame des Victoires) to invoke the Christ. "But the Christ is no more!" I said to myself.

---

[20]Black sun: associated with Dürer's Angel of Melancholia. Victor Hugo, in his great poem "Ce que dit la Bouche d'ombre," would write of a "terrible black sun which radiates night" at the very time (1854) when Nerval was writing *Aurélia*.

[21]Moons passing at great speed: Rimbaud records a similar hallucination, induced by a powerful narcotic.

"They don't know it yet." The invocation lasted an hour or so. Finally I got up and went out for a walk, beneath the arcades of the Palais-Royal. I told myself that the sun probably had enough light left to illuminate the earth for three days, but that it was using up its own substance, and indeed it did look cold and pale to me. Eating a cookie to allay my hunger and give me strength, I went to the German poet's house. Upon entering, I told him that it was all over, that we must all prepare to die. He called in his wife, who said: "What's the matter with you?" "I don't know," I said. "I am doomed!" She sent for a fiacre, and had a young girl take me to the Dubois Clinic.

V

There, my malady continued in various alternative forms. A month later I was released, apparently back to normal. In the two months that followed, I resumed my peregrinations in the environs of Paris. The longest trip I made was to visit the cathedral of Reims. Little by little I started writing again, and finished one of my best novellas.[22] The writing, however, was accomplished laboriously, almost always in pencil on loose sheets of paper, at odd moments when I was not wandering about or preoccupied by my daydreaming. Making corrections agitated me a great deal. A few days after publishing this novella, I began to suffer from persistent insomnia. I would prowl Mont-

---

[22]*Sylvie*, written and published in 1853. A major influence on Proust. Bettina L. Knapp: "*Sylvie*, one of the most exquisite prose works in French literature, is considered by men of letters a superb example of French 'clarity of expression.' Paradoxically, it was written at a time when Nerval was a victim of schizophrenia."

martre all night and then watch the sunrise from the top of
the hill. I would have long talks with peasants and laborers.
At other times I would go to the city market. One night I had
supper in a boulevard café and amused myself by tossing
gold and silver coins in the air. Then I went to the market
and got into an altercation with a stranger, whose face I
slapped very hard; I don't know why this never had any
repercussions. Upon hearing the clock of Saint-Eustache
strike a certain hour, I started thinking about the battles
between the Burgundians and the Armagnacs, and thought
I saw the ghosts of combatants of that era rising up all
around me. I picked a quarrel with a parcel-carrier wearing
a silver plaque on his chest, who I said was the duke Jean de
Bourgogne. I kept trying to prevent him from entering a
cabaret. For some reason which I cannot explain, when he
saw that I was threatening his life, tears began to stream
down his face. This touched me, and I let him pass.

I walked down to the Tuileries, which were closed, along
the quays bordering the river, and up to the Luxembourg;
then I came back to have lunch with a friend of mine. After
that I went to Saint-Eustache, where I knelt piously at the
altar of the Virgin, thinking of my mother. The tears I shed
eased my soul; and on my way out of the church I bought a
silver ring. From there, I went to visit my father, but he was
out; so I left a bouquet of daisies at his house. From there I
went to the Jardin des Plantes. It was crowded with people,
and I spent some time watching the hippopotamus bathe in
its pool. Then I went in to view the osteology galleries.
Seeing those monstrous bones made me think of the flood,
and when I came out it was pouring rain. I thought: "Bad
luck! All these women and children are going to get wet!"
Then I said to myself: "But it's much more than that.
Actually, it's the beginning of the great deluge!" The water
was rising in all the neighboring streets; I ran down the Rue

Saint-Victor, and with the idea of stopping what I believed to be a universal inundation, I threw into the deepest spot the ring I had purchased at Saint-Eustache. At almost that very moment the rain stopped, and a ray of sunshine broke through the clouds.

Hope returned to my soul. I was supposed to meet my friend Georges at four o'clock, and I set out for his lodgings. Stopping in at a curio shop on the way, I bought two velvet screens covered with hieroglyphic inscriptions. It seemed to me that these were the consecration of Heaven's pardon. I reached Georges' house exactly on time, and confided my hopefulness to him. I was wet and tired. I changed clothes and lay down on his bed. In my sleep, I had a marvelous vision. It seemed to me that the Goddess appeared to me, saying: "I am the same as Mary, the same as thy mother, the same also as that one whom thou hast always loved, in all her forms. In each of thy trials, I have taken off one of the masks I wear to veil my features, and soon thou shalt see me as I really am." A delightful orchard emerged from the clouds behind her, a soft but penetrating light illuminated this paradise, and all the while I heard nothing but her voice; but I felt myself plunged into a pleasant euphoria. — Shortly afterward I awoke and said to Georges: "Let's go out." As we were crossing the Pont des Arts, I explained the transmigration of souls to him, and said: "It seems to me that tonight I have within me the soul of Napoleon, inspiring me and commanding me to do great things." In the Rue du Coq I bought a hat, and while Georges was collecting the change for the gold piece I had tossed onto the counter, I went on ahead to the arcades of the Palais-Royal.

There, it seemed as if everyone was looking at me. A persistent notion had lodged itself in my mind: that there were no dead any more. I wandered through the Galerie de Foy saying: "I've made a mistake"; but I was unable to determine what the mistake was by consulting my memory, which I believed was that of Napoleon . . . "There's something around here that I haven't paid for!" I entered the Café de Foy with this idea in my head, and I thought I recognized one of the habitués as Père Bertin of the *Débats*.[23] Then I strolled through the garden area and took some interest in watching the little girls play ring-around-the-rosy. After that I left the arcades and made my way to the Rue Saint-Honoré. I stepped into a shop to buy a cigar, and when I came out, the crowd in the street was so dense that I felt almost suffocated. Three friends of mine extricated me, taking responsibility for me, and took me into a café to wait while one of them went for a fiacre. I was taken to the Hospice de la Charité.

During the night my delirium increased, especially after midnight when I realized that I was under physical restraint. I managed to get out of the strait-jacket, and toward morning went for a walk about the halls. Believing I had become god-like and had the power to cure illness, I laid hands on several patients, and approaching a statue of the Virgin, I took her crown of artificial flowers to strengthen this power I believed I had. I went striding along, talking animatedly about the ignorance of men who thought they could heal the sick by science alone; and espying a small bottle of ether on a table, I drained it at a single draft. A young intern, whose face seemed to me to be that of an angel, tried to stop me; but nervous energy made me strong, and just as I was about to knock him down, I refrained, telling him that he did not understand what my mission was. Some doctors arrived on the scene, and I resumed my discourse on the impotence of their profession. Then I went out the street

---

[23]Père Bertin. The reader is referred to Ingres' magnificent portrait.

door and down the steps, notwithstanding the fact that I was barefooted. Coming to an ornamental flower-bed, I stepped into it and picked some flowers, walking on the forbidden grass to do so.

One of my friends had come back to get me. So I stepped out of the flower-bed, and as I was talking to him, a strait-jacket was thrown around my shoulders; then I was put into a fiacre and driven to an asylum outside of Paris. When I saw that I was among the insane, I realized that everything up to that point had been nothing but an illusion. Still, it seemed to me that the promises which I attributed to the goddess Isis[24] were being fulfilled through a series of trials I was destined to undergo; so I accepted them with resignation.

The part of the asylum in which I found myself overlooked a broad promenade shaded by walnut trees. In one corner there was a little hillock where one of the inmates walked around in a circle all day long. The rest, including me, contented themselves with walking about on the raised terrace, which was bordered by a steep grassy embankment. On one wall, situated on the west side, some figures had been drawn, one of which represented the man in the moon, with geometrical lines for the eyes and mouth; onto this face someone had painted a kind of mask; the wall at the left had on it several drawings in profile, one of which appeared to be a sort of Japanese idol. Farther on, a death's-head had been gouged into the plaster; on the opposite wall, two freestones had been sculpted by some denizen of the place into grotesque little masks, rather well rendered. There were two doors leading to cellars, and I imagined these to be subter-

---

[24]Isis. An Egyptian goddess, sister and wife of Osiris, mother of Horus, and goddess of Nature

ranean passages like the ones I had seen at the entrances to the Pyramids.

VI

At first I imagined that the persons assembled in this garden all had some kind of influence on the heavenly bodies, and that the one who kept walking constantly around in a circle was regulating the motion of the sun. An old man who was brought in at certain hours of the day, and who kept tying knots and consulting his watch, appeared to me to be keeping a record of the passage of time. To myself I attributed an influence over the behavior of the moon, and I believed that a thunderbolt, visited upon that heavenly body by the Almighty, had left on its face the mask-like imprint I had observed.

I attributed mystical meaning to all words spoken by the attendants and by my companions. It seemed to me that the latter were there as representatives of all the races on earth, and that we were supposed to establish a new pattern for the movement of the heavenly bodies and to develop the system more fully. It was my belief that an error had crept into the overall scheme of numbers, and that this was the source of all the troubles of mankind. I believed moreover that certain celestial spirits had assumed human form and were attending this general congress, while seeming to be engaged in mundane pursuits. My own role seemed to me to be to reestablish universal harmony by cabalistic art, and to seek solutions by invoking the occult powers of all the various religions.

In addition to the outdoor promenade, we also had a common room or hall whose perpendicularly-scored windows overlooked a vista of greenery. When I gazed at the row of outbuildings beyond those windows, I fancied I could see outlined the many-windowed façades of a thousand pavilions adorned with arabesques and surmounted by fretwork and needle-tipped spires,[25] reminding me of the imperial *kiosques* on the shores of the Bosporus. This naturally set me to thinking about Oriental matters. At about two o'clock I was given a bath, and it seemed to me that I was being served by the Valkyries, daughters of Odin, who were endeavoring to elevate me to immortality by removing from my body, little by little, all its many impurities.

In the evening, my soul at peace, I took a walk in the moonlight, and when I raised my eyes to the trees, it seemed to me that the leaves moved about capriciously in such a way as to form images of cavaliers and ladies on caparisoned horses.[25] For me, these were the triumphant figures of my ancestors. This thought led me to another: that there was a great conspiracy afoot among all animate beings to restore the world to its primordial harmony, and that communications about this were taking place via the magnetism of the heavenly bodies; that an unbroken chain around the earth linked together the intelligences devoted to this general communication, and that songs, dances and glances were magnetized messages between one individual and another, conveying the same aspiration. The moon was for me the refuge of fraternal souls who, delivered from their mortal bodies, were working more freely toward the regeneration of the universe.

For me, each day's time now seemed to be augmented by two hours; so that when I got up in the morning at the time fixed by the asylum's clocks, all I seemed to be doing was

---

[25]These images of Oriental architecture and of figures seen in windblown leaves parallel those induced by hashish, opium and mescalin.

moving about in the realm of the spirits. The companions around me seemed to be entranced, soulless figures, like the specters of Tartarus,[26] until the hour when the sun rose for me. Then I would greet that heavenly body with a prayer, and my real life would begin.

From the moment when I became certain that I was being subjected to certain trials as a sacred rite of initiation, a feeling of invincibility came over me. I deemed myself a hero living under the watchful eye of the gods; all things in nature took on new aspects, and secret voices spoke to me from plants, trees, animals, even the humblest insects, to inform and encourage me. In my companions' speech there were mysterious turns of phrase whose secret meaning I was able to comprehend; objects without form or life lent themselves voluntarily to my mental calculations: from the configuration of pebbles, from the shape of corners, cracks or apertures, from the indentations of leaves, from colors, odors and sounds, I saw emerge hitherto-unrecognized, harmonious patterns. "How," I said to myself, "can I have existed so long out of touch with nature, and without identifying myself with it? All things live, function, relate to one another; the rays of magnetism emanating from myself or from other individuals pass without impediment along and through the endless chain of created things; they form an invisible network which covers the whole globe, and detached filaments of them make their way by degrees to the very planets and stars. Captive for the time being on the earth, I am in touch with the sun, the moon and the stars, who share in my joys and my sorrows!"

At once I trembled, to think that this very mystery could

---

[26]Tartarus. A region of Hades to which the greatest sinners and blasphemers were consigned.

be fathomed. "If electricity," I said to myself, "which is the magnetism of physical bodies, is subject to a control which imposes laws upon it, there is all the more reason to believe that hostile, domineering spirits can reduce other intelligences to slavery and can use their own divided strength against them to achieve domination over them. This is how the ancient gods were conquered and enslaved by new gods; this is how," I continued to myself, consulting my recollections of the ancient world, "the necromancers seized power over whole races of people who have remained, generation after generation, captive subjects of their eternal despotism. Even Death itself, alas, cannot set them free! For we live again in our sons as we have already lived in our fathers, and our enemies, with their ruthless science, know how to recognize us everywhere. The time of our birth; the point on earth at which we appear; our first gesture; the name, the chamber, and all the rites and sacraments which are imposed upon us—all this establishes a serial pattern, either auspicious or calamitous, on which our future wholly depends. But if this is so terrible in terms of purely human calculations, think what its effect must be on the mysterious formulæ which establish the order of the worlds! What has been said is true: there is nothing in the universe that is indifferent, nothing that is powerless; an atom can disintegrate everything, an atom can save anything!

"O terror! There it is, the everlasting distinction between good and evil. Is my soul an indestructible molecule, a little globule inflated by a bit of air but destined to regain its place in nature, or is it that perfect emptiness, the image of nothingness, which will disappear into infinity? Could it be moreover the doomed part, the part destined to suffer, in all its transformations, the punitive vengeance of the powers that be?" I felt compelled to take stock of my life, and even of my previous existences. By proving to myself that I was good, I proved to myself that I must always have been so. "And if I have been wicked," I said to myself, "will not the life I am now leading be a sufficient atonement?" This thought reassured me a little, but it did not dispel my fear of being consigned forever to the ranks of the wretched. I felt as though I had been plunged into cold water, and sweat, even colder, trickled from my brow. I turned again in my thoughts to the eternal Isis, the sacred wife and mother; all my hopes and prayers merged into that magical name; I felt myself coming alive again in her, and sometimes she appeared to me in the guise of the Venus of antiquity, sometimes also with the features of the Christians' Virgin. That night brought this dear apparition back to me more distinct than ever before, and yet I said to myself: "What can she do, defeated and perhaps oppressed as she is, for her poor children?" Pale and tattered, the crescent moon was growing thinner every night and would soon disappear; perhaps we were never again to see it up there in the sky! It seemed to me, however, that that heavenly body was the refuge of all souls akin to mine, and I saw it as peopled with plaintive spirits destined to be reborn one day on earth . . .

My room is at the end of a corridor with the inmates living on one side and the asylum's domestic servants on the other. Mine is the only room privileged to have a window facing the tree-shaded courtyard which serves as our promenade in the daytime. My gaze lingers with pleasure on a thick-foliaged walnut tree and two Chinese mulberries. Beyond these one can barely discern, through lattices painted green, a rather busy street. To the westward, the horizon opens out: it's like a small town, with house-windows framed by greenery or obstructed by bird cages and drying laundry; every now and then there appears the profile of some housewife, young or old, or the rosy face of a child. There is shouting, singing, loud laughter; this can be merry or sad to listen to, depending on the time of day and one's state of mind.

I have found here in my room all the debris of my diverse fortunes, a hodgepodge of items left over from several sets of furnishings dispersed or sold in the course of the past twenty years. It's a capernaum like that of Dr. Faust. An antique three-legged table with eagle-heads; a console supported by a winged sphinx; a seventeenth-century commode; an eighteenth-century bookcase; a bed of the same period, the oval ceiling of its canopy (as yet unmounted) lined with red *lampas*; a rustic étagère laden with pieces of stoneware and Sèvres porcelain, most of them rather badly damaged; a narghile brought back from Constantinople; a large alabaster cup; a crystal vase; some wooden panels, from the demolition of an old house I once lived in on the site of the Louvre, and covered with mythological paintings done by friends of mine who are now famous; two large canvases in the Prud'hon style, representing the Muses of history and drama. I have spent several very pleasant days arranging all this, creating in this cramped attic space a bizarre ensemble which has about it something of the palace and of the cottage, and which sums up rather well my roving existence. I have hung up above my bed my Arab garments, my two assiduously-mended cashmeres, a pilgrim's calabash, and a hunter's game-bag. Above the bookcase is displayed a large-scale plan of Cairo; a bamboo console at the head of my bed holds a lacquered tray from India on which I can arrange my toilet articles. I am very glad to have about me these humble relics of my years of alternating good fortune and wretchedness, linked as they are with all the memories of my past life. The only things missing, put aside for me,[27] are a small painting on copper in the style of Correggio,[28] representing *Venus and Cupid*; some pierglasses depicting huntresses and satyrs; and an arrow which I had kept as a souvenir of the Valois archery clubs I had belonged to in my boyhood. (My guns were sold when the new laws went into effect.) In short, I have found here almost everything I owned when I came here. My books, a bizarre accumulation of the learning and knowledge of all eras: history, travel, religions, cabala, astrology—a conglomeration to gladden the hearts of Pico della Mirandola, the sage Meursius and Nicholas of Cusa—the Tower of Babel in two hundred volumes—they have let me have it all! There is enough here to drive a wise man mad; we shall see whether there is also enough to make a madman wise.

What a pleasure it has been to have the chance to organize and file in drawers my voluminous notes and letters, personal or public, obscure or noteworthy, depending on what persons I chanced to encounter or what distant countries I traveled in! In rolls more carefully wrapped than the others, I find letters written in Arabic, souvenirs of Cairo and Istambul. O joy! O mortal sorrow! This faded handwriting, these scribbled first drafts, these half-crumpled letters—here is the treasure trove of my only love . . . Let's read it all through once more . . . Many of the letters are missing, many others torn across or full of crossed-out passages; here is what I find:

. . . .

One night, I was talking aloud to myself and singing, in a kind of ecstasy. One of the attendants came to my cell to get me and took me down to a room on the ground floor,

---

[27]These were articles of metal or glass, potentially dangerous in the hands of a mentally deranged person.

[28]Correggio. An Italian painter (1494-1534).

where he locked me in. Although standing up, I went right on dreaming; it seemed to me that I was confined in a kind of Oriental pavilion. I inspected every corner of it and found that it was octagonal. A padded seat extended around the walls, and it appeared to me that the latter were of thick ice, through which I could see brilliant jewels, shawls and tapestries on the other side. Through the grillwork of the door I could discern a moonlit landscape, and I seemed to recognize the shapes of the tree-trunks and the rocks. I must have sojourned there in some other existence, and I thought I recognized the deep grottoes of Ellorah. Gradually a bluish daylight seeped into the pavilion and caused bizarre images to appear. Then I thought I was in the middle of a vast charnel-house where the history of the universe was being written in blood. On the wall opposite me was painted the body of a gigantic woman, its parts all severed as if by a saber; on the other walls, more women of diverse races, their bodies growing ever larger and more dominant, appeared in a bloody tangle of members and heads—from empresses and queens to the humblest of peasant women. This was a comprehensive history of crimes, and all I had to do was to fix my eyes on any particular spot, to see another tragic scene being enacted there. "This is the result," I said to myself, "of the bestowal of power upon men. Bit by bit, men have destroyed and cut up into a thousand pieces the eternal essence of beauty, with the result that the races of mankind are becoming more and more diminished in strength and physical perfection . . ." And I could actually see, threading its way through one of the apertures in the door, a shadowy procession of the declining generations of future races.

At last I was distracted from this somber contemplation. The kind, compassionate face of my excellent doctor restored me to the world of the living. He took me with him to witness a spectacle which interested me greatly. Among the patients was a young man, a former soldier from Africa, who for six weeks had been refusing to take any nourishment. By means of a long rubber tube introduced into his stomach, he was being forced to swallow nutritive liquids. In addition to this, he could neither see nor speak.

This spectacle made a strong impression on me. Absorbed thus far in the monotonous cycle of my own feelings or mental agonies, I found here an indefinable, enigmatic being, silent and long-suffering, sitting like a sphinx at the supreme portals of existence. I began to love him for his state of wretchedness and abandonment, and I felt myself uplifted by this feeling of sympathy and pity. Situated thus halfway between life and death, he seemed to me a kind of sublime interpreter, a confessor predestined to hear those secrets of the soul which the spoken word would not dare convey or could not successfully render. He was the ear of God, without any admixture of another person's thought. I spent whole hours mentally examining myself, with my head bent over his and his hands in mine. It seemed to me that there was a certain magnetic force uniting our two spirits, and I was absolutely delighted when, for the first time, a word came out of his mouth. People just couldn't believe it; and I attributed this beginning of a cure to my having willed it so ardently. That night I had a delightful dream, my first such dream in a very long time. I was in a tower, dug so deeply into the earth and soaring so high into the sky that my whole existence seemed destined to be consumed in climbing up and down. My strength had already flagged and I was about to lose heart, when a side door suddenly opened; a spirit appeared and said to me: "Come, brother! . . ." For some reason, it occurred to me that his name was Saturnin. His features were those of the poor patient, but transfigured and intelligent. We were out in open country, at night, with the stars shining brightly above us. We stopped to contemplate this spectacle, and the spirit put his hand on my forehead, as I had done the day before in seeking to magnetize my companion; thereupon one of the stars I saw in the sky began to grow larger, and the female Deity of my dreams appeared to me, smiling, dressed in an almost Indian costume, as I had seen her long before. She walked between us, and the fields turned green, and flowers and vegetation sprang up from the ground wherever her feet had trod . . . She said to me: "The trial thou hast undergone is now ended; those countless staircases so exhausting for thee to climb or descend were the very bonds of the illusions which once confused thy thinking; and now, think back to that day when thou didst implore the Holy Virgin, and believing she was dead, suffered seizure of thy mind by delirium. It was essential that thy plea be conveyed to her by a simple soul, untrammeled by the bonds of earth. Such a person has been found in thy company, and this is why it has been granted that I come here in person to encourage thee." The joy which this dream diffused within my spirit afforded me a rapturous awakening. Dawn was just breaking. I wanted to have some material evidence of the apparition which had so comforted me, and I wrote on the wall these words: "Thou didst visit me last night."

I am recording here, under the heading of *Memorabilia*, what I recall of several dreams which succeeded the one just reported.

MEMORABILIA

Atop a steep mountain in Auvergne, the shepherds' song rang out. Poor Mary! Queen of the heavens! It is you whom they are piously addressing. That rustic melody struck the ear of the Corybants, priests of Cybele.[29] They emerged, also singing, from the secret grottoes where Love had made shelters for them. — Hosanna! Peace on earth and glory in the heavens!

On the Himalayan mountains a little flower was born. — "Forget me not!" —The sparkling glance of a star fixed itself upon her for a moment, and a reply made itself heard, in a melodious alien tongue: *"Myosotis!"*

A silver pearl glittered in the sand; a golden pearl sparkled in the sky ... The world was created. Chaste loves, divine sighs—inflame the sacred mountains!... for you have brothers in the valleys and timid sisters who steal away to the deep woods!

O fragrant groves of Paphos,[30] you cannot match those dear retreats where the lungs are filled with the life-giving air of the Homeland. — "Up there in the mountains—the people live content; — the nightingales' wild music—means happiness to me!"

Oh, how wonderful is my great friend! She is so great that she pardons the whole world, and so good that she has pardoned me. The other night, she was lying abed in some palace or other, and I could not get to her. My burnt-chestnut horse kept slipping out from under me. The broken reins hung loose over his sweaty rump, and I had to work very hard to keep him from lying down on the ground.

Last night, good Saturnin came to my aid, and my great

---

[29]Cybele. A Phrygian goddess, called by the Romans the Great Mother. Edith Hamilton: "... the Corybantes ...worshiped her with cries and shouts and clashing cymbals and drums."

[30]Paphos. A city named after the son of Pygmalion and Galatea.

friend stationed herself at my side, on her white mare caparisoned in silver. She said to me: "Courage, brother! This is the final phase." And her great eyes devoured space, and her long hair, impregnated with all the perfumes of Yemen, began to stream out behind her in the air.

I recognized the divine features of Aurelia. We were flying to our triumph, and our enemies were at our feet. The bird of passage was guiding us to the highest heaven, and the bow of light flashed in the divine hands of Apollo. The enchanted horn of Adonis sounded through the forests.

"O Death, where is thy victory," since the conquering Messiah was riding between the two of us? His robe was of sulphurated hyacinth, and His wrists and ankles glittered with diamonds and rubies. When His light riding-crop touched the mother-of-pearl gates of the New Jerusalem, all three of us were inundated with light. It was then that I descended among men to announce to them the glad tidings.

I just had a very sweet dream: I saw again the woman I had loved, all transfigured and radiant. The heavens opened to me in all their glory, and there I read the word *pardon* written in the blood of Jesus Christ.

A certain star suddenly began to glow, and it revealed to me the secret of the world and of the universe. Hosanna! Peace on earth and glory in the heavens!

From the bosom of silent darkness two notes rang out, one low-pitched, the other high, — and at once the eternal orb began to spin. Be blessèd, O prime octave, first sweet note of the divine anthem! Entwine together all our days, from Sunday to Sunday, in your magical fabric! The hills sing you to the valleys, the springs to the brooks, the brooks to the rivers, and the rivers to the Ocean; the air stirs, and light dances in harmonious patterns among the budding flowers. A trembling sigh of love escapes the swollen breast of the earth, and the heavenly choir of the stars stretches away into infinity; it contracts, expands, moves off, approaches, — and it scatters far and wide the seeds of new creations.

On the summit of a bluish mountain a little flower was born. — "Forget me not!" The sparkling glance of a star fixed itself upon her for an instant, and a reply was heard in a musical, alien tongue: *"Myosotis!"*

Woe to you, god of the North,[31]— you who shattered with a blow of your hammer the Sacred Table, wrought of the seven most precious metals! For you could not shatter the *Pink Pearl* which lay in the center of the table. It rebounded under the blow of the iron—and lo, we have armed ourselves for its sake . . . Hosanna!

The *macrocosm*, or great world, was constructed by cabalistic art; the *microcosm*, or little world, is the image thereof, reflected in all hearts. The Pink Pearl was tinted with the royal blood of the Valkyries. Woe to you, O smith-god, who did attempt to shatter a world!

Nevertheless, Christ's pardon has also been proclaimed for you!

Be you also blessed, O Thor the giant—most powerful of the sons of Odin! Be blessed in Hela, your mother, for death is often sweet, —and in your brother Loki,[32] and in your dog

---

[31]Thor. The Norse god of thunder.

Garm![33]

The very serpent which encompasses the earth is also blessed, for it relaxes its coils, and its gaping maw inhales the scent of the anxoka flower, the sulphured flower, —the dazzling flower of the sun!

May God preserve the divine Balder,[34] son of Odin, and Freya[35] the beautiful!

I found myself *in spirit* at Saardam, which I had visited last year. There was snow on the ground. A very small girl, slipping now and then on the frozen ground, was making her way toward the house of Peter the Great. Her profile had something of Bourbonian majesty about it. Her neck and throat, brilliantly white, were partially revealed by a palatine of swan plumes. She was carrying a lighted lamp, shielding it from the wind with her little pink hand; and she was about to knock on the green door of the house, when a thin, bony cat came out of it and entangled itself in her legs, causing her to fall down. "Well! It's only a cat!" said the little

---

[32]Loki. The son of a giant; caused much mischief to the Norse gods.

[33]Garm. In Norse mythology, the dog that guards the gate to the Kingdom of Death, ruled by the goddess Hela.

[34]Balder. Most beloved of the Norse gods. Loki killed him with a sprig of mistletoe, after disguising himself as a woman and learning from Balder's mother Frigga that this was the one thing which could harm her son.

[35]Freya. Norse goddess of Love and Beauty, who had the right, along with the Valkyries, to claim her share of the dead after a battle. Freya means Friday.

girl, getting to her feet. "Even a cat is something!" a soft voice replied. I was present at this scene, and I was carrying on my arm a small gray cat, which began to mew. "It's that old fairy-woman's child," said the little girl.

And she went into the house.

Last night my dreams took me first to Vienna. — It is common knowledge that on each of that city's public squares, tall columns called pardons have been erected. Around these are clustered marble figures representing the Solomonic order[36] and supporting spheres where seated divinities preside. All of a sudden, wonder of wonders, I began thinking of that majestic sister of the Emperor of Russia whose imperial palace I had seen at Weimar. Next, a bittersweet melancholy gave rise to a vision of the tinted mists of a Norwegian landscape in a soft grey daylight. Then the clouds became transparent, and I saw falling away before me a deep chasm into which the icy waters of the Baltic were tumultuously plunging. It appeared that the river Neva, with its blue waters, would be engulfed entirely in this global fissure. The ships in the harbors of Kronstadt and St. Petersburg were straining at their moorings, on the point of breaking away and disappearing into the chasm, when this scene of desolation was suddenly illuminated from above by a divine light.

As that bright light penetrated the fog and mist, I saw appear at once the rock on which stands the statue of Peter

---

[36]Solomon, the King of Israel, was reputed to have power over certain demons. The Sign of Solomon, made by joining the thumbs and the first two fingers of the hands at the tips to form the Star of David, robbed such demons of their earthly disguise.

the Great. Above that firm pedestal, clouds began to gather, rising to the zenith. They were laden with radiant, divine figures, among whom could be distinguished the two Catherines and the empress Saint Helen, as well as the most beautiful princesses of Muscovy and Poland. All were gazing benevolently, through long glass telescopes, in the direction of France. From this I gathered that our country was to become the arbiter of the eastern dispute[37] and that they were awaiting resolution of that quarrel. My dream ended in the sweet expectation that peace would at last be granted us.

All this was my way of carrying on a boldly conceived endeavor. I had resolved to fix my dreams clearly in my memory and to discover their hidden meaning. I said to myself: "After all, why not force my way through those mystic gates, armed with all my strength of will, and master my feelings instead of yielding to them? Is it not possible to tame this fascinating awesome chimera, to exert some control over these spirits of the night who make a mockery of our human reason? One third of our life is spent in sleep. It is consolation for the troubles of our waking hours or atonement for their pleasures; but I have never experienced sleep to be mere repose. After a few minutes' lethargy, a new life begins, untrammeled by the limitations of time and space, and undoubtedly similar to that which awaits us after death. Who knows whether or not there may be a linkage between these two existences, and whether or not it is already possible for the soul to establish that relationship?

---

[37]The "eastern dispute" is the Crimean War (1853-1856).

From that moment, I tried very hard to comprehend the meaning of my dreams, and this anxious state of mind had its effect on my reflections whenever I lay awake. I fancied I understood that a linkage really did exist between the inner and the outer world; that it was only inattention or mental disorder which rendered obscure the obvious relationship between them; and that this explained the bizarre quality of certain dream tableaux—like distorted, grimacing reflections of real objects moving about on the surface of troubled waters.

Such matters as these were my nighttime preoccupation; my days were spent quietly in the company of the unfortunate patients, who had become my friends. The realization that I was henceforth cleansed of all the transgressions of my past life gave me infinite mental satisfaction and pleasure; certitude of my own immortality and of the coexistence of all the persons I had loved had come to me, as it were, in a material, tangible way, and I blessed the brotherly soul who had rescued me from the depths of despair and brought me back into the luminous pathways of religion.

The poor fellow from whom intelligent life had been so singularly withdrawn was given attention and care which, little by little, triumphed over his torpor. Having learned that he was country-bred, I spent whole hours singing to him old village songs, with as much feeling and expression as I could muster. I had the good fortune to observe that he heard and understood these songs and even repeated parts of them to himself. One day, at long last, he opened his eyes for just a moment, and I saw that they were blue, like those of the spirit who had appeared to me in dreams. One morning, a few days later, he opened his eyes wide and did not close them again. He also began talking, but only at intervals; he recognized me, addressed me as "thou" and called me brother. One day, coming in from the garden, he said to me: "I'm thirsty." I fetched him a drink; his lips touched the glass, but he could not swallow. "Why," I said to him, "will you not eat and drink like the rest of us?" "Because I am dead," he said; "I was buried in such-and-such cemetery, in plot number so-and-so." — "And now, where do you think you are?" — "In purgatory. I am performing my atonement."

Such are the bizarre ideas which maladies of this kind induce; I acknowledged inwardly that I had been very near to believing things just as strange about myself. The treatment I had received had restored me to the affection of my family and friends, and I was now able to consider more rationally the world of illusions in which I had lived for a considerable time. Nevertheless, I am happy with the firm convictions I have acquired, and I compare this series of trials I have undergone to what used to be represented, for the ancients, by the idea of a descent into Hell.

Sylvie

$\mathcal{M}$EMORIES OF $\mathcal{V}$ALOIS[1]

I
Sleepless Night

I was coming out of a theater where I used to show up every night, dressed to the nines like a suitor, to occupy a front seat in the mezzanine, overlooking the stage.[2] Sometimes there was a full house, sometimes the hall was half empty. I took no special interest or pleasure in contemplating an orchestra section occupied sparsely by a few dozen hard-core theater-goers, and loges by women in old-fashioned hats and dresses—nor even in being part of an animated, rustling hall, ringed at all levels by flowered gowns, sparkling jewels and radiant faces. Indifferent to the spectacle within the hall, I was almost equally so to that on the stage—until the moment when, in the second or third scene

---

[1][All serially-numbered footnotes to this translation are the work of Eric Basso. The translator's own notes are identified by an asterisk.] Nerval may have begun work on *Sylvie* as early as the summer of 1852. The novella was published on August 15, 1853 in the *Revue des Deux Mondes*. Valois, a region of northern France known for its lush vegetation, made famous by the pastoral writings of Rousseau.

[2]The story is set in the 1830s, when Nerval worked as a drama critic.

of some deadly-dull masterpiece of the day, a figure well known to me would appear, filling all empty space with light, and with a word or a sigh restoring life to those insignificant figures around me.[3]

I felt that my life was being lived in her, that she existed for me alone. Her smile filled me with infinite bliss; the sound of her voice, so soft yet of such distinctive timbre, made me tremble with joy and love. To me, she was perfect in every way; she was the answer to all my yearnings, the subject of all my fantasies—beautiful as day when the footlights illumined her from below, pale as a moonlit night when the footlights went down and left her lighted more naturally by the chandeliers, glowing in the dark with a beauty all her own, like the divine Hours which stand out, each with a star in its forehead, against a dark background in the frescoes of Herculaneum!

A year had passed, and I had not even considered trying to find out what kind of person she might be; I was reluctant to disturb the magic mirror in which I saw her image reflected; at the very most, I had heard a few comments concerning her—the woman, not the actress. I paid as little attention to them as I would have to rumors about the Princess d'Elide or the Queen of Trébizonde—an uncle of mine, who had lived through the late years of the 18th century, having warned me long ago that actresses were not real women, and that nature had neglected to give them a

---

[3]Nerval haunted the Variétés and the Opéra-Comique, theaters where Jenny Colon performed in operetta from 1834 to 1836. In the beginning, he admired her from afar. Later, they became friends. Gérard did his best to promote Jenny's career in his review, *Le Monde Dramatique,* on which he squandered the remains of the inheritance his grandfather had left him. Jenny married a flutist in 1838, and died in 1842. Gérard's grand passion for Jenny Colon grew into an obsession which survived her death and played no small part in unhinging his mind.

heart. No doubt he was talking about the actresses of his own day; but he had told me so many stories of his illusions and disillusionments and had shown me so many portraits on ivory, charming medallions that he later used as decoration for tobacco-boxes, so many yellowed *billets*, so many faded favors, meanwhile telling me in detail the whole history of each, that I had become accustomed to thinking ill of all actresses, without making allowance for changing times.

At that time we were living in a peculiar era, one of those which seem to follow revolutions or the downfall of great reigns. It was no longer an age of heroic gallantry as under the Fronde, nor of elegantly-clad vice as under the Regency, nor of skepticism and wild orgies as under the Directoire; for us it was a mélange of activity, indecision and laziness, of sparkling utopias, philosophic or religious aspirations and vague enthusiasms, mingled with certain instinctive impulses toward renaissance; a time of ennui with old quarrels and contentions, of hopeful uncertainty—something like the eras of Peregrinus and Apuleius.[4] The materialistic man was smelling roses, anticipating his regeneration by the hand of Isis the Beautiful;[5] that chaste goddess, forever young, would appear to us in dreams at night and reproach us for having wasted our waking hours. But our youth was not a time of

---

[4]Peregrinus, Greek philosopher (? - 165 A.D.). He adopted Christianity, then abandoned it in favor of the Cynic philosophy. Peregrinus attempted to incite a revolt against Rome, then threw himself onto his own funeral pyre at Olympus before a stunned crowd. Lucius Apuleius, Roman satirist and philosopher (fl. 2nd century A.D.). Though most of his writings were scientific and philosophical treatises, he is remembered for his mystical satire, *The Golden Ass*, a tale of sorcery, seduction, metamorphosis and redemption.

[5]Isis, Egyptian moon goddess, wife and sister of Osiris (god of fertility), and mother of Horus. From the scattered pieces of her husband's body, she and her sister Nephthys fashioned the first Egyptian mummy.

great ambitions, and the frantic pursuit of position and honors kept us out of potential spheres of activity. Our only refuge was the ivory tower of the poet, in which we climbed higher and higher to isolate ourselves from the crowd. At these great heights to which our mentors led us, we breathed at last the pure air of solitude, quaffed forgetfulness from the golden cup of legend, and became intoxicated with poetry and love. Love, alas, of certain forms and shapes, of certain shades of pink and blue, of metaphysical phantoms! Seen at close range, any real woman was revolting to us, in our ingenuosness; a woman had to appear to be a queen or a goddess, and above all to be untouchable.

Some of us, however, not totally inhibited by these platonic paradoxes, would sometimes brandish over our Alexandrian[6] dream-world the torch of the underworld gods, which can illuminate the darkness for an instant with its trails of sparks. — So it was that upon coming out of the theater bitterly saddened as always by the evanescence of my dreams, I would hie myself with alacrity to a certain club, where I would mingle with the company and have supper, and where all melancholy would be dissipated by the irrepressible verve and repartee of some brilliant intellects — keen, tumultuous, at times sublime — minds such as have always been in evidence during times of regeneration or of decadence, and whose debates sometimes became so vociferous that the more reserved among us would tiptoe to the windows to see whether the Huns, Turks or Cossacks might be arriving to cut short the arguments of the rhetoricians and sophists.[7]

---

[6]Alexandria, capital of Egypt and site of the greatest of ancient libraries.

[7]Henri Lemaitre: ". . .one of the literary and artistic coffeehouses of the romantic period, the *Café de Valois*."

"Let us drink and make love; therein lies wisdom!" That was the universally-held opinion among the younger set. One of them said to me: "For a long time now, I've been running into you at the same theater, every time I go there. *Which one* are you after?"

Which one? To me, it did not seem possible that one could be going there for *another*. I did, however, confess to a certain name. "Well!" said my friend indulgently. "See that fellow over there? He's the lucky dog who just escorted her home, and who, according to the rules of our club, won't be seeing her again, perhaps, until this night is over."

Without too much emotion, I looked in the direction of the person indicated. He was a young man, correctly dressed, somewhat pale and nervous-looking, with proper manners and gentle, melancholy eyes. He was tossing gold coins onto a whist table and losing them with apparent indifference. "What do I care," I said, "if it's he or someone else? There had to be someone, and that fellow looks worthy enough of having been chosen."

"And what about you?"

"Me? I'm pursuing a vision, that's all."

On my way out I passed through the reading room, and automatically glanced at a newspaper. My object, I think, was to see what was going on in the financial world. Amid the debris of my former opulence there was a considerable sum in foreign securities. A rumor had been circulating that after having been considered worthless for a long time, these securities were going to be re-accredited — and this had just occurred, following a change of ministries. Their value per share was already up very high; I was becoming rich again.

This change in my situation brought to my mind a single, overwhelming thought: namely, that the woman I had loved for so long was now mine, if I wanted her. — My ideal was within reach of my hand. But was this not just another illusion—a misprint, or some kind of hoax? No, the other newspapers were telling the same story. — The sum of money I had gained loomed up before me like the golden statue of Moloch. I thought: "What would that young man in there say now, if I were to go and usurp his place beside the woman he has left alone?" ... I trembled at the thought, and my pride rebelled.

No! Not that way! At my age, one does not kill love with money; I will not be a corrupter. Besides, this is an idea left over from another era. Who is to say this woman is venal? — In glancing at random through the newspaper I was still holding, I came upon these two lines: *"Provincial Fête of the Bouquet. — Tomorrow, the archers of Senlis are to return the bouquet to those of Loisy."* These simple words triggered in my mind a whole series of remembered impressions; they were a reminder of my long-forgotten provincial life, a distant echo of innocent feast-days of my early youth. — The horn and the drum resounded afar in hamlets and woodlands; young girls were weaving garlands, singing, and matching the colors of bouquets of flowers with festive ribbons. — A heavy wagon drawn by oxen was being loaded with presents as it moved along, and we children of the region were walking in procession with our bows and arrows, each of us labeled with the name of some titled knight — not realizing that we were merely repeating, from age to age, an old Druidic rite which had survived monarchies and new religions.

II
Adrienne

I went home to bed, but was unable to get any rest. As I lay immersed in semi-somnolence, all my youthful days passed in review through my mind. This physical state, in which the mind is still resistant to the bizarre associations of dreams, often enables a person to see again, condensed into a few minutes' time, the most salient tableaux of a long period of his life.

My mind's eye saw again a castle of the time of Henri IV, with its slate-roofed, pointed towers and its reddish façade quoined in yellow stone, and near by a great open greensward surrounded by elm and linden trees, their foliage pierced through by the fiery rays of a setting sun. On the greensward a number of girls were dancing in a circle and singing old songs taught them by their mothers, the words in such a pure, natural French that the hearer was acutely conscious of being in old Valois, where the heart of France has been beating for more than a thousand years.

I was the only boy in that circle, having been brought along by Sylvie, a little girl from a neighboring village who was my dearest companion. How fresh and vivacious she was, with her dark eyes, classic profile and lightly-tanned complexion! I loved only her, had eyes only for her—until that day! I had scarcely noticed, in our group dancing the *ronde*, a tall, beautiful blonde girl named Adrienne. All of a sudden, as we followed the prescribed pattern of the dance, I found myself alone with Adrienne in the center of the circle. We were of the same height. We were told to kiss, and the dancing and singing whirled on faster than ever. As I gave her that kiss, I could not resist squeezing her hand. The long, rolled curls of her golden hair brushed my cheek. From that moment on, I felt a strange sort of agitation coming over me. —The beauty was supposed to sing, in order to have the right to go on dancing. We all sat down around her, and she began at once, in a fresh, strong, resonant voice, slightly husky as is common among girls in this foggy country, to sing one of those old ballads of love and melancholy, recounting the misadventures of a princess who is locked up in her tower by a strong-willed father as punishment for having fallen in love. Each line of the song ended with those quavering trills which are so effectively executed by young voices, when they are imitating the quavering sound of old people's voices in a modulated tremolo.

As she sang, it grew very dark under and around the great trees, and the light of a new moon fell upon her, standing there all alone within our listening circle. When she stopped singing, no one dared break the silence. The greensward was now overspread by condensed light moisture, covering the tips of the grass-blades with flecks of white. We felt as if we were in Paradise. At length I arose and ran to the parterre of the castle, where there were some potted laurel trees in large, monochrome porcelain urns. I brought back two sprigs of laurel, which were woven into a crown and tied with a ribbon. This ornament I placed on the head of Adrienne, its lustrous leaves glistening on her blond hair in the pale moonlight. She looked like Dante's Beatrice smiling at the itinerant poet as they neared the holy dwelling-places. Drawing herself up to her full height, she made a graceful gesture of farewell and ran back into the castle. — She was, we were told, the granddaughter of a living descendant of a certain family related to some former kings of France; the blood of the House of Valois flowed in her veins. For this fête, she had been permitted to take part in our activities; we were to see her no more, for the next day she left for the convent in which she was a student-boarder.

When I came back to where Sylvie was, I saw that she was crying. The crown presented by my hand to the beautiful singer was the cause of those tears. I offered to get more branches and make another crown for her; but she said she didn't care for that idea at all, since she had no right to wear a crown. In vain did I try to justify myself; she said not a single word to me all the way home to her parents' house.

Upon returning to Paris to resume my studies, I carried

with me these ambivalent feelings: regret and sorrow for the end of a loving friendship, counterbalanced by a vague, impossible new love, the source of some mental anguish which textbook philosophy was powerless to relieve.

The figure of Adrienne eventually emerged victorious — a mirage of glory and beauty, sharing my hours of serious study or tempering their austerity. At vacation time the following year, I learned that the beauty I had had such a brief glimpse of had become a nun, dedicated by her family to the religious life.

III
Resolution

All was made clear to me by this half-dreamed memory. This vague, hopeless love for a woman of the theater, which would come over me at curtain-time and would not leave me until I fell asleep at night, had had its origin in my remembrance of Adrienne, a night-blooming flower in the pale moonlight, a pink-and-gold phantom gliding over green grass bathed in white vapors. The image of that face of hers, forgotten for years, suddenly became and remained singularly clear in my mind; it was as if a pencil-drawing blurred by time had become a painting, like one of those old sketches by master painters once admired in a museum, which one recalls later upon seeing elsewhere the dazzling masterpiece it foreshadowed.

In love with a nun, in the body of an actress! . . . And suppose the two were the same woman! — It's enough to drive one mad! It's a fatal allurement, drawing me on and on in pursuit of the unknown, like a will-o'-the-wisp fleeing over the reeds of a stagnant pond. . . But let's get our feet back on solid ground.

And what of Sylvie, whom I once loved so much? Why had

I forgotten her for three whole years? . . . She was such a pretty girl, the prettiest in Loisy!

No doubt she's still there, still innocent and pure of heart. I can still see her window where the grapevine and roses entwine, with the cage of warblers hanging at the left; I can still hear the musical sound of her spindles, and her favorite song:

> The beautiful lady sat
> Beside the flowing brook. . .

She's still waiting for me. . . Poor as she is, who would have married her? Would she have married some rough-handed, sunburnt-faced peasant in overalls, from her own or a neighboring village? She loved only me, the little Parisian who came from time to time to visit my poor uncle, now dead, who lived near Loisy. For three years I have been living like a lord, dissipating the modest sum of money he left me, which could have been enough to last me a lifetime. With Sylvie, I would have saved my money. Now good fortune has given some of it back to me. There is still time.

At this hour, this moment, what is she doing? Sleeping... No, she is not sleeping; today is a feast day, the fête of the bow, the only day of the year when people dance all night. She's at the fête.

What time is it?

I had no watch.

Among all the splendid bric-à-brac it was then customary to collect in order to restore some local color to a very old apartment such as mine, there gleamed with revived brilliance one of those Renaissance shell clocks whose gilded dome, surmounted by the figure of Time, is supported by Medici-style caryatids, which in turn rest on semi-rearing horses. The Diana of legend,[8] leaning on her stag, is in bas-

---

[8]Diana, also called Artemis. Edith Hamilton: "She was the Lady of Wild Things, Huntsman-in-Chief to the gods, an odd office for a woman."

relief on the dial, where the enameled numbers of the hours are displayed on a niello background. The movement, probably a fine one, had not been wound for some two hundred years. — When I bought that clock in the Touraine, it was not because I expected it to tell me the time.

I went downstairs to the concierge's apartment. His cuckoo-clock showed one o'clock in the morning. "In four hours," said I to myself, "I can be in Loisy for some dancing." There were still five or six fiacres on the Place du Palais-Royal, waiting for habitués of the clubs and gambling-houses. "To Loisy!" I said to the nearest driver.

"Where's that?"

"Near Senlis, eight leagues."

"I'll take you to the mail-coach station," said the driver, who was less preoccupied than I.

What a dreary road at night, that Flanders highway! Not until it enters the forested areas does it become beautiful. Those two monotonous rows of trees go on and on, vague shapes grimacing; beyond them, rectangles of green and of plowed land, bounded on the left by the bluish hills of Montmorency, Écouen, Luzarches. New here is Gonesse, an ordinary-looking town rich in memories of the Holy League and the Fronde. . .[9]

---

[9]Holy League, *La Ligue*. Founded in 1576, under the aegis of Henri, Duc de Guise (a Roman Catholic leader in the infamous Massacre of Saint Bartholomew), for the suppression of the Calvinists. King Henri III, driven from his throne by the rebel duke, had him assassinated in 1588, only to be assassinated himself a year later by a Dominican friar. Twice defeated in battle by Henri IV, the discredited and unpopular Holy League was finally disbanded in 1594. The Fronde: two revolts against the boy-king Louis XIV. The first uprising (1648-49) was led by the Paris *parlement*, and involved the middle class and part of the nobility; the second (1651-52), largely a matter of political intrigue, pitted mutinous nobles, led by the young king's cousin Le Grand Condé, scheming ladies of the royal court, and the army against Cardinal Mazarin, who had thrown Condé, a popular military hero, into prison because he feared his power. Mazarin and the royal family were driven from Paris, and Condé freed from prison, but the second Fronde soon petered out.

Beyond Louvres there is a road lined with apple trees, whose blossoms I have seen many times gleaming in the darkness like earthborn stars; that used to be the shortest route to the villages. —Now, while the coach is climbing these hills, let me reconstruct and organize my recollections of the days when I used to come up here often.

IV
A Voyage to Cythera[10]

Several years had elapsed; my encounter with Adrienne in front of the castle was by this time no more than a childhood memory. Again I found myself at Loisy on the feast-day of the patron saint. Again I joined the knights of the bow, taking my place in the same company I had previously belonged to. The fête had been organized by some young members of the old families who still owned several of the old castles deep in the forests of the region, castles which had suffered more from the passage of time than from revolutions. From Chantilly, Compiègne and Senlis, joyous cavalcades came to take their place in the time-honored procession of the bow companies. After the long parade through villages and towns, the mass in the church, and the games and contests of skill, the winners of the latter received their prizes and were thereupon invited to a repast which was to be enjoyed on an island, shaded by poplars and

---

[10]Remembered today chiefly by Watteau's famous painting, *L'Embarquement pour l'Ile de Cythère* (1717) and *L'Isle joyeuse* (ca. 1904), the Debussy piano piece which evokes it, Cythera was also the site of Francesco Colonna's mystical marriage to the Principessa Lucrezia Polia, recounted in his *Hypnerotomachia Poliphili* (Poliphilo's Dream), published in 1499, a book — or, more precisely, an incunabulum — whose influence on Nerval was decisive. The sea-birth of Venus occurred off the Island of Cythera.

lindens, in the middle of one of the small lakes fed by the Nonette and the Thève. Boats decked out in flags and bunting took us to the island, — the choice of which had been determined by the existence there of an oval temple with columns, which was to serve as a dining room for the banquet. The area around Loisy, like that around Ermenonville, is bestrewn with such small late-eighteenth-century edifices, the tastes prevalent in that period having served as inspiration for their builders, some of whom were millionaire philosophers.

I believe this particular temple had initially been dedicated to Urania.[11] Three of its columns had fallen down, carrying with them a section of the architrave; but the interior of the enclosure had been cleared and garlands hung between the columns, rejuvenating this modern ruin—one which suggested the paganism of Boufflers or Chaulieu rather than that of Horace.[12]

The lake-crossing had perhaps been conceived as imitating Watteau's painting *Voyage à Cythère*.[13] Only our modern attire marred the illusion. The huge feast-day bouquet was lifted off the wagon that had been carrying it and placed on a large boat; the young girls dressed in white, who accompanied it according to custom, took their places on the thwarts, and this graceful *theoria*[14] performed as in ancient times

---

[11]Urania, the Muse of astronomy.

[12]Stanislas-Jean, Chevalier de Boufflers (1738-1815), cavalry officer and author of light verse, now mercifully forgotten. Guillaume Amfrye, Abbé de Chaulieu (1639-1720), a refined, and dissolute, society poet and free-thinker. His later work expresses a weariness with the *beau monde* and is tinged with melancholy. "Fontenay" and "La Retraite" are among his principal poems. Horace, Roman poet (65-8 B.C.). Among his works are the *Satires*, *Odes* and *Ars Poetica*.

[13]*Sic*. See note 10.

[14]*Theoria*, procession.

was reflected in the calm waters separating it from the shore of the island, which was quite colorful in the evening sunlight with its hawthorn copses, its colonnade and its bright green foliage. Within a short time all the boats reached the shore. The ceremonial flower-basket occupied the center of the table, and each person took his seat, those most favored alongside girls, provided the former were known to relatives of the latter. The result of this was that I found myself once again beside Sylvie. Her brother had already joined me, during the fête; he reproached me for not having visited his family for a long time. I apologized for this, saying that my studies had kept me in Paris, and assured him that this time I had come with just such a visit in mind. "No," said Sylvie, "I'm the one he has forgotten. After all, we're just village folk, and Paris is so far above us!" I tried to close her mouth with a kiss; but she was still sulky with me, and her brother had to intervene before she would deign, with an air of indifference, to offer me her cheek. I took no pleasure in that kiss; it was a favor shared by many others, for in this patriarchal land where any passer-by rates a warm greeting, a kiss between individuals is nothing more than an act of courtesy.

A surprise had been arranged by the organizers of the fête. When the meal was over, out from the bottom of the huge basket flew a wild swan, held captive until that moment under the flowers; with his strong wings beating, he lifted up the tangled mass of garlands and wreaths and scattered them in all directions. As he flew off joyously toward the last gleams of the setting sun, we began catching wreaths at random, each of us adorning therewith the brow of the girl next to him. I was lucky enough to catch one of the most beautiful wreaths, and Sylvie, with a smile, allowed herself to be kissed, more tenderly this time than before. It was clear to me that by doing this I was effacing the memory of a former time. This time I admired her with undivided

attention; how beautiful she had become! She was no longer
that little village girl I had slighted in favor of someone taller
and more accomplished in social graces. Everything about
her had progressed: the charm of her dark eyes, so seductive
even when she was a child, had become irresistible; beneath
her well-arched eyebrows, her smile, suddenly lighting up
those serene, classically regular features, had something
Athenian about it. I marveled at that physiognomy worthy
of Greco-Roman art, contrasting with the pleasant but
irregular features of her companions. Her delicately tapered
hands, her whiter, more rounded arms, her supple figure, all
combined to make her look quite different to my eyes. I could
not resist telling her how different I found her from her
former self, hoping this would cast a different light on my
earlier lack of constancy and mitigate its damage.

Furthermore, I had everything in my favor; her brother's
friendship, the delightful atmosphere of the fête, the evening
hour, and even the pleasant surroundings in which those
elegant solemnities of olden days had been so faithfully
reproduced, in such a thoroughly tasteful and imaginative
way. As often as we could, we slipped away from the dancing
to reminisce together about our childhood memories and to
gaze dreamily at the many colors of the sky and their
reflections on the foliage and the water. It took Sylvain,
Sylvie's brother, to tear us away from that contemplation; he
told us it was time to return to the village where their
parents lived, some distance away.

V
The Village

Their home was in Loisy, in what had once been the
game-keeper's lodge. I accompanied them there, then started

back to Montagny to my uncle's house, where I was staying. Upon leaving the road to cross a small woodland separating Loisy from Saint-S...*, I soon found myself following a narrow footpath that skirts the forest of Ermenonville; I was expecting this to take me to the walls of the convent, which I would then follow for a quarter of a league. The moon, appearing from time to time from behind the clouds, faintly illuminated the dark sandstone boulders and the clumps of heather and gorse I was making my way through. To my left and right lay patches of trackless woods, and farther on, some of the Druidic stones which in that region make one think about the sons of Armen[15] exterminated by the Romans! From atop these lofty stone-piles I could see the lakes in the distance, like shining mirrors in contrast to the foggy plain; but I was not able to identify precisely the one where the fête had taken place.

The night air was warm and balmy; I resolved to go no farther, but to await the morning, and I made my bed on some tufts of heather. — Upon awakening, I recognized one by one various landmarks around this spot to which I had wandered during the night. To my left I could make out the long line of the convent wall of Saint-S..., then on the other side of the valley the Butte des Gens-d'Armes with the jagged ruins of its ancient Carolingian residence. Near by, rising above some patches of woodland, the tall structures of the Abbaye de Thiers loomed on the horizon, with their sections of wall pierced by cloverleaf- and ogive-shaped apertures. Farther on, the Gothic manor-house of Pontarmé, surrounded by water as of old, soon reflected the first rays of the morning sun, while to the south rose the tall keep of the Tournelle and the four towers of Bertrand-Fosse, on the lower slopes of Montméliant.

---

*Convent of Saint-S. . . .: probably Saint-Sulpice.

[15]Armen, a Gallic chieftain.

The previous night had been a very sweet one for me, and my thoughts were all of Sylvie; but when I saw the convent, the idea struck me that it might be the one in which Adrienne was living. The ringing of its morning bell, still echoing in my ear, was probably what had awakened me. For a moment I thought about having a look over the wall by climbing some rocks to their highest point; but upon reflection, I rejected the idea as a profanation. The light of day, growing stronger, drove that vain memory from my thoughts and left therein only the rosy-pink features of Sylvie. "Let's go wake her up," I said to myself, and started back toward Loisy.

Here now is the village, at the end of the footpath which skirts the forest: a score of cottages, their walls festooned with grapevines and climbing roses. A group of early-morning spinners are at work together in front of one of the cottages. Sylvie is not among them. She is now almost a young lady of quality, since she has become a maker of fine lace, whereas her relatives have remained simple village folk. —I went up to her room without surprising anyone; long since out of bed, she was manipulating her lace-making spindles, which clicked softly over the square of green cloth in her lap. "So there you are, lazybones!" she said, with her heavenly smile. "I'm sure you've just left your bed!" I told her about my sleepless night spent stumbling about among the trees and rocks. For a moment she made an effort to feel sorry for me. "If you're not completely tired out, I'm going to have you do some more running. Shall we go see my great-aunt in Othys?" When I consented, she immediately arose, went to her mirror, arranged her hair and put on a rustic straw hat, her eyes sparkling with innocence and happiness. We set out, following the banks of the Thève, through fields dotted with daisies and buttercups, then along the Saint-Laurent forest, sometimes taking short-cuts across brooks and through thickets. Blackbirds whistled in the trees, and tom-tits flitted cheerfully in and out of the bushes disturbed by our passing.

At times we found ourselves walking through periwinkles, those flowers so dear to Rousseau, displaying their blue corollas among their long, creeping branches with paired leaves, like small vines, which kept catching at the flying feet of my companion. Indifferent to these reminders of the Genevese philosopher, she kept searching here and there for fragrant strawberries, while I talked to her about *La Nouvelle Héloïse*, reciting several passages from memory. "Is that pretty language?" she asked.

"It's sublime."

"Better than Auguste Lafontaine?"[16]

"It's more refined, more sensitive."

"Oh!" she said. "I'll have to read that. I'll tell my brother to get it for me the next time he goes to Senlis."

And I continued to recite excerpts from the *Héloïse* while Sylvie went on picking strawberries.

VI
Othys

Upon emerging from the woods, we came across some large clumps of purple foxglove; she made an enormous bouquet of it, saying to me: "It's for my aunt; she'll be so happy to have these beautiful flowers in her bedroom." We had left only a bit of level terrain to cross to reach Othys. The village's church-steeple jutted up above the low-lying bluish hills between Montméliant and Dammartin. Once again the Thève was gurgling along among its boulders and pebbles, a much smaller stream up here near its source, where it rests

---

[16]Auguste Lafontaine (1758-1831), a popular German novelist of the period.

for a while in the fields, forming a small lake bordered by gladioli and iris. Soon we came to the first houses. Sylvie's aunt lived in a little cottage built of irregular chunks of sandstone and thoroughly covered with trellises and arbors bearing grape- and hop-vines; she lived alone, and since the death of her husband, the people of the village had been cultivating for her the several plots of land she still owned. For her, the arrival of her niece was like "fire in the house." "Good morning, Auntie! Your kids are here!" said Sylvie. "We're really hungry!" She embraced her tenderly, put the bouquet of flowers into her hands, then finally remembered to introduce me, saying: "This is my sweetheart!"

I embraced the aunt in my turn, and she said: "He's very nice . . . and a blond, too!"

"He does have pretty hair," said Sylvie.

"That doesn't last," said the aunt, "but the two of you have plenty of time, and since you're a brunette, you and he make a well-matched couple."

"We've got to feed him, Auntie," said Sylvie; and away she went, rummaging in cupboards and bread-bin, collecting milk, brown bread and sugar, and setting the table in a not-too-neat fashion with porcelain plates and serving-dishes bearing glazed designs with big flowers and roosters with bright plumage. A Creil porcelain pitcher full of milk with strawberries floating in it became the centerpiece, and after raiding the garden for a few handfuls of cherries and currants, she anchored each end of the tablecloth with a vase of flowers. But the aunt had spoken these beautiful words: "All that stuff is nothing but dessert. Now you must let me take over." With that she had taken down the skillet from its hook and tossed a piece of firewood into the big fireplace. "I don't want you touching this!" she said to Sylvie, who was trying to help her. "You'll hurt those pretty fingers of yours that make such beautiful lace, better than Chantilly! You've given me some of it, and I know what I'm talking about."

"Oh, all right, Auntie! By the way, if you have any really old pieces, I could use them as patterns."

"Well now," said the aunt, "go upstairs and look. There may be some in my chest of drawers."

"Give me the keys."

"Don't be silly!" said the aunt. "The drawers are open."

"That's not so; there's one that's always locked." And while the good woman was cleaning the skillet after having heated it in the fire, Sylvie detached from the key-ring at her waist a little wrought-iron key, which she held up triumphantly to show me.

I followed her as she climbed quickly up the wooden stairs to the bedroom. — O blessèd youth, O sainted age! — Who in the world would have dreamed of besmirching the purity of a first love in that memory-filled sanctuary of wedded bliss? From a gilded oval frame hanging at the head of the rustic bed, the portrait of a young man of the good old days, with dark eyes and pink mouth, smiled at us. He wore the uniform of a game-keeper of the House of Condé;[17] his semi-martial pose, his rosy-cheeked, benevolent look, his clear white forehead beneath the powdered hair, all made this perhaps mediocre pastel quite remarkable in its youthfulness and simplicity. Some minor artist invited to the princely hunts had done his very best to portray the subject as faithfully as possible; he had done the same for the young man's bride, in another picture we found in a locket—alluring, mischievous, tall and slender in an open-bodiced dress adorned with a ladder of horizontal ribbons, and teasing with pursed lips a bird perched on her finger. And this was the very same good-hearted old woman who at that moment was downstairs cooking, bent over the hearth fire. That made me think of the Ropewalker fairies, who conceal beneath their wrinkled masks an attractive face, which they

---

[17]House of Condé: a collateral branch of the royal family. See note 9.

reveal at the dénouement, when the Temple of Love appears with its spinning sun beaming with magical lights. "Sweet Auntie," I cried, "how pretty you were!"

"And what about me?" said Sylvie, who had managed to open that famous drawer. She had found therein a long dress of flame-colored taffeta whose folds made a rustling sound. "I want to see how this would look on me," she said. "Ah! I'm going to look like a fairy, an old-time fairy!"

"The ever-young fairy of the legends!" said I to myself. Sylvie had already unhooked her calico dress and was letting it fall to her feet. Her aunt's ample gown fell into place perfectly on Sylvia's slim figure, and she told me to hook it up in the back. "Oh —flat sleeves! How ridiculous!" she said. But the lace-trimmed cuffs set off her bare arms admirably; her bosom was well framed by the plain bodice with its yellowed lace netting and ribbons, which had encased her aunt's vanished charms only a very few times. "Come on, get it done!" Sylvie said to me. "Don't you even know how to hook up a dress?" She looked like Greuze's *Accordée de village*.[18]

"You should have some powder," I said.

"We'll find some." She rummaged again in the drawers. Oh, what riches! How good it all smelled, that mass of cheap finery gleaming, sparkling, shimmering with color! Two rather dilapidated mother-of-pearl fans, some papier-mâché boxes with Chinese pictures painted on them, and hundreds of baubles, frills and furbelows, among them two little white drugget shoes, their buckles encrusted with Irish diamonds!* "Oh!" said Sylvie, "I want to put those on, if I can find the embroidered stockings!"

A moment later we had found and were unfolding some

---

[18]*Accordée de village* (Betrothed Village Girl), by Jean-Baptiste Greuze (1725-1805), popular painter of sentimental portraits and tableaux.

*Drugget: a thick, heavy fabric woven of hair, wool, cotton, jute, etc. Irish diamonds: undoubtedly rhinestones.

sheer silk stockings, rose-colored embroidered in green; but the voice of the aunt, accompanied by the crackling sound of the skillet, abruptly called us back to reality. "Go on down, quick!" said Sylvie; and despite all my pleas, she refused to let me help her put on the shoes and stockings. Meanwhile the aunt had just turned out into a serving-dish the contents of the skillet: a rasher of bacon fried with eggs. Soon Sylvie's voice called me back upstairs. "Quick, put those on!" she said, now fully dressed and pointing to the gamekeeper's wedding clothes, laid out on top of the chest. In a trice, I transformed myself into a bridegroom of the previous century. Sylvie waited for me on the stairs, and we went down together, holding hands. The aunt, turning around, cried out: "Oh, my dear children!" and began to cry, then smiled through her tears. —We were a picture from her youth — a cruel, haunting apparition! We sat down beside her, touched and almost solemn; but our gaiety was soon restored, for after that first moment, the good old woman could talk of nothing but her memories of her wedding-day celebration. She even remembered the chants in concert, customary in those days, which were repeated responsively from one end of the nuptial table to the other, and the simple epithalamium recited by all present as the wedded couple went back indoors after the dancing was over. Sylvie and I repeated together those unsophisticated, rhythmic lines, with their traditional pauses and assonances, tender and eloquent as the canticles of Ecclesiastes;—for one entire summer evening, we were bride and groom.

VII
Châalis

It's four o'clock in the morning; the road plunges down into a fold of the terrain, then climbs up again, on its way through Orry to La Chapelle. On the left we pass a road that skirts the edge of the Hallate woodland. That's the road Sylvie's brother took me over in his buggy one evening, for a very special event. It was on a St. Bartholomew's Eve, I believe. His little horse went flying through the woods like a witch, over one little country road after another. At Mont-l'Evêque we rejoined the main road, and a few minutes later pulled up at the gamekeeper's lodge of the ancient Abbaye de Châalis. —Châalis! Another memory!

This old retreat of emperors has nothing left to impress the visitor except the ruins of its cloister, the last row of its Byzantine arcades still standing silhouetted against the ponds—a forgotten relic of the religious establishments forming a part of those domains once called "Charlemagne's farms." Religion, in this area isolated from the bustle of highways and towns, has conserved some elements reminiscent of its long occupancy by cardinals of the Este family, in the era of the Medici; its attributes and practices still have something gallant and poetic about them, and one breathes an aura of the Renaissance under the chapel arches with their finely-decorated ribbed vaulting, painted by artists from Italy. The faces of saints and angels stand out in pink against the delicate blue of the vaults, with touches of pagan allegory that bring to mind the sentimentalities of Petrarch and the fabulous mysticism of Francesco Colonna.[19]

We were interlopers, Sylvie's brother and I, at the unusual spectacle which was taking place that evening. A very high-born person, the owner of the property at that time, had had the idea of inviting several families of the region to a kind of allegorical dramatic performance in which some nuns from a nearby convent were to appear. This was nothing like the tragedies of Saint-Cyr; it dated back to the

[19]Francesco Colonna. See note 10.

earliest lyrical efforts imported into France in the Valois era. What I saw performed was like a *mystère* of ancient times. The costumes consisted of long robes, varying only in color: they were all azure, hyacinth or dawn. The characters were angels, and the action took place amid the debris of a world in ruins. Each angel voice would sing of one of the splendors of this extinguished globe, and the Angel of Death would respond by citing the reasons for that splendor's destruction. One angelic spirit rose up from the abyss, brandishing a flaming sword, and summoned the others to come and witness the glory of Christ, conqueror of the nether world. That spirit was Adrienne, transfigured by her costume as she had already been by her vocation. To us, the gilded-cardboard halo encircling her angelic head seemed really to be a circle of light; her voice had increased in strength and in range, and the endless flourishes of Italian song embroidered with their bird-like warblings the solemn phrases of a serious, ceremonious *recitativo*.[20]

As I recall to mind the following details, I am wondering whether they are real, or whether I dreamed them. Sylvie's brother was a bit tipsy that evening. We had stopped for a few moments at the gamekeeper's lodge — where, much to my surprise, there was a flying swan on the door, then, inside the lodge, some tall armoires of carved walnut, a tall clock in its case, and some bows and arrows mounted like trophies above a red-and-green shooting-license. A queer-looking dwarf with a monkey on his head,* holding a bottle in one hand and a ring in the other, seemed to be inviting the archers to take careful aim. This dwarf, I believe, was cut out

---

[20]*Recitativo*, opera dialogue sung between the arias.

*The phrase *coiffé d'un bonnet chinois* could of course be read as "wearing a Chinese cap"; but since *bonnet chinois* is the common name for a species of monkey, the bonneted macaque, the latter is probably what this odd-looking cutout dwarf had on his head.

of sheet metal. But was the appearance of Adrienne as real as these details, as real as the undeniable existence of the Abbaye de Châalis? At any rate the gamekeeper's son really did show us into the hall where the performance was taking place; we were near the door, at the rear of a large audience, seated and deeply moved. It really was St. Bartholomew's Day—singularly linked to the memory of the Medici, whose coat of arms coupled with that of the House of Este adorned those old walls. Could this memory be only a figment of my imagination?—Fortunately, here we are now, stopping at the Le Plessis road, where I leave the coach; I escape from the world of reverie and dreams, and I have left only a quarter-hour's walk to reach Loisy, by some paths that show signs of infrequent use.

VIII
The Loisy Dance

I arrived at the Loisy dance at that melancholy, still-quiet hour when lights are turning pale and trembling at the approach of day. The tops of the linden trees were taking on a bluish cast, lighter than their underparts. The rustic flute was no longer getting so much competition from the trilling of the nightingale. Everyone looked pale, and I had difficulty finding any familiar faces among the depleted groups of dancers. At last I espied a tall girl named Lise, a friend of Sylvie's. She gave me a kiss. "We haven't seen you around here in a long time, Parisian!" she said.

"Yes, it has been a long time."

"And you've just arrived?"

"Yes, by the mail coach."

"And none too soon!"

"I wanted to see Sylvie. Is she still here?"

"She never leaves till morning, she's so keen on dancing."

A moment later, I was at her side. She looked tired, but those dark eyes still shone with that old Athenian smile of hers. There was a young man standing near her. She signaled to him that she was not dancing the next quadrille. He withdrew, with a bow.

Dawn was breaking. We left the dance, holding hands. Sylvie's hair was undone, the flowers in it all askew; the nosegay at her bosom was shedding petals on the crumpled lace, some of her own fine handiwork. I offered to see her home. It was full daylight by now, but the weather was threatening. On our left the Thève went murmuring along, leaving at every bend an eddy of quiet water where yellow and white water-lilies were in bloom, an embroidery of delicate water-stars shining like daisies. The fields were bestrewn with bundles and stacks of hay, whose odor went to my head without making me drunk, as the fresh scent of woods and copses of flowering hawthorn used to do.

It didn't occur to us to go walking in the woods again. "Sylvie," I said to her, "you don't love me any more!" She sighed.

"My friend," she said, "we must face facts; things just don't happen as we want them to in life. In the old days you used to talk to me about *La Nouvelle Héloïse*; I read it, and I trembled as I came upon this sentence at the very beginning: 'Any young girl who reads this book is lost.' But I disregarded that, trusting in my own good sense. Do you remember the day we put on my aunt's wedding clothes? ... The illustrations in that book also showed the lovers wearing old-fashioned clothes; so for me you were Saint-Preux, and I saw myself in Julie. Why, oh why, didn't you come back then? But you were in Italy, it seems. You must have seen girls down there a lot prettier than I!"

"Not one, Sylvie, who had your eyes and your pure classic features! You are a nymph of antiquity, and don't realize it!

Furthermore, things in this part of the world are just as beautiful as they are in the Roman countryside. Those granite crags over there are no less sublime than those of Terni, and there's a similar cascade falling from the high rocks. I saw nothing down there that I might miss, living here."

"What about Paris?" she said.

"In Paris. . ." I shook my head, without replying.

All of a sudden I thought of the futile, obsessive vision that had been bewildering me for so long.

"Sylvie, please," I said. "Do you mind if we stop here?"

I threw myself at her feet, weeping hot tears; I confessed all my doubts, my indecisions, my sudden impulses; I evoked the baneful apparition that was permeating my whole life. "Save me!" I added. "I'm coming back to you, for always."

She turned to face me, her eyes filled with pity. . .

At this moment, our private talk was interrupted by a burst of uproarious laughter. It was Sylvie's brother, coming to join us with the good-natured rustic gaiety inevitably brought on by an all-night fête, and rendered excessive in his case by frequent liquid refreshment. He was calling out to Sylvie's escort of the evening, who was off somewhere in the hawthorn bushes and soon appeared, to join us. This lad was just about as unsteady on his feet as his friend, and he seemed even more embarrassed by the presence of a Parisian than by that of Sylvie. His open, candid physiognomy, his air of deference mingled with embarrassment, made it impossible for me to hold it against him that he was the dancer for whom Sylvie had stayed so long at the fête. I judged him to be not very dangerous as a rival.

"We have to go home," said Sylvie to her brother. To me she said, "See you later!" and offered me her cheek to kiss. The Romeo took no offense.

IX
Ermenonville

Not being at all sleepy, I went to Montagny to have a look at my deceased uncle's house. A great sadness came over me as I caught my first glimpse of its yellow façade and green shutters. Everything seemed to be just as it had always been, —but I had to go to the tax-assessor's house to get the door key. Once the shutters were opened, I noted with some emotion that the old furniture had been kept in good condition, having been polished from time to time: a tall walnut armoire; two Flemish paintings said to be the work of an ancestor of ours, a former artist; some large prints in the Boucher style, and a whole framed series of Moreau engravings from *Emile* and *La Nouvelle Héloïse*; on the table, a stuffed dog whom I had known in life, a former companion of my wanderings in the woods, —perhaps the last of the pug-dogs, the now-extinct breed to which he belonged.

"As for the parrot," said the tax-assessor, "he's still alive; I took him home with me."

The garden was a glorious conglomeration of wild vegetation. In one corner I recognized a child's garden that I myself had once planted. Trembling with emotion, I entered my uncle's study, where still to be seen were the little bookcase full of choice books, old friends of their now-departed owner, and on the desk some antique artifacts found in his garden: vases, Roman medallions, etc., —a local collection in which he used to take great pleasure.

"Let's go see the parrot," I said to the tax-assessor. The parrot was demanding his lunch, just as in his younger days, and he stared at me with his round eye set in wrinkled skin, which reminded me of the wise, experienced look of an old man.

Filled with the melancholy thoughts evoked by this belated return to such well-loved places, I felt the need to see the face of Sylvie again; she was the only young, vital person who might reestablish my ties to this region. I set out again for Loisy. It was midday, and everyone was asleep, tired out by the fête. So it occurred to me to amuse myself by taking a walk to Ermenonville, a league away by the forest road. The summer weather was fine. From the start I took pleasure in the coolness of that route, which is like an *allée* in a park. The uniform green of the great oaks was varied only by the white trunks of birches, with their trembling leaves. The birds were still; I heard only the sound of green woodpeckers hammering out nest-holes in the trees. Once I came close to losing my way, for in some places the markers indicating the various routes are not clear, some of their letters having been effaced. At last, leaving the Wilderness on my left, I reached the dancing-circle, where the sculpted bench for older people still stands. All the atmosphere of philosophic antiquity, recreated by the onetime owner of the estate, came back to me in a rush in the presence of this picturesque realization of *Anacharsis* and *Emile*.[21]

When I saw the waters of the lake gleaming through the branches of willow and hazel, I recognized unmistakably a spot to which my uncle had taken me many times on our walks together: the *Temple of Philosophy*, which its builder had unfortunately been unable to complete. Shaped like the temple of the sibyl Tiburtine, and still standing within its sheltering grove of pines, it bears the names of all those great philosophical thinkers beginning with Montaigne and Descartes and ending with Rousseau. This unfinished edifice is by now no more than a ruin; ivy festoons it gracefully, and brambles invade its disjointed steps. There, as a child, I witnessed ceremonies in which young girls dressed in

---

[21]*Voyage du jeune Anacharsis en Grèce* (1788), by L'Abbé Jean-Jacques Barthélemy (1716-1795), set in the 4th century B. C.; and *Emile*, the famous novel by Rousseau.

white came up to receive prizes for their studies and their good behavior. Where are the rosebush hedges that used to encircle the hillock? What's left of them, a few plants reverting to the wild state, is overrun by eglantine and raspberry canes. —As for the laurels, have they been cut down, as in the song about the girls who won't go to the woods any more? No, those shrubs of sunny Italy have simply died, done in by our foggy climate. Fortunately, Virgil's privet is still blooming, as if to underscore the words of the master inscribed above the portal: *Rerum cognoscere causas!*[22] —Yes, the temple is falling down, like so many others; oblivious or weary men will ignore, avoid and neglect it; an indifferent Nature will take back the terrain which Art had sought to lay claim to; but the thirst for knowledge will remain eternal—the fountainhead of all power and all activity!

Here is the island with its poplars, and here the tomb of Rousseau, now empty of his ashes.[23] O sage, you once fed us the milk of the strong, but we were too weak to profit from it! We have forgotten those precepts of yours which our fathers used to know; we have lost the thread of your discourse, a final echo of the wisdom of the ages. Yet let us not despair, and like you at your supreme moment, let us turn our eyes toward the sun!

Once again I saw the castle, the peaceful waters beside it, the cascade murmuring over the rocks, and the causeway

---

[22]"To learn the causes of things." Publius Vergilius Maro (70-19 B. C.), known as Virgil, author of the *Aeneid*, greatest of Roman epics, also wrote pastoral verse, collected in the *Eclogues*, and the *Georgics*, whose themes include agriculture, animal husbandry and bee-keeping.

[23]When Rousseau died in 1778, he was buried at Ermenonville, on the Isle of Poplars. His remains were disinterred in 1794 and taken to Paris, where they were entombed in the Panthéon near those of Voltaire. In May 1814, supporters of the Bourbon Restoration secretly entered the Panthéon, dug up the bones of Voltaire and Rousseau, stuffed them into a sack and buried them in a dump outside Paris. The remains were never found.

with four dovecotes marking its corners that joins the two
parts of the village; the lawn extending far beyond like a
savannah, bordered by shady hillsides; Gabrielle's[24] tower is
reflected from a distance in the waters of an artificial lake
dotted with ephemeral flowers; foam bubbles up, insects
hum... One must beware and avoid the noxious gas emitted
when water comes in contact with the powdery sandstones
of the wilderness and the sandy moors, where pink heather
contrasts with green bracken. How lonely and sad it all is!
Sylvie, when she used to come with me to these places, lent
them a special charm with her obvious delight, her mad
dashing here and there, her shouts of joy. She was still a
wild, barefoot child, her skin bronzed despite her straw hat
with its wide ribbon flying helter-skelter amid her long black
tresses. We would go to the Swiss farm to get a drink of milk,
and people would say to me: "How pretty she is, that
sweetheart of yours, little Parisian!"

No country bumpkin could have danced with her then!
She would dance only with me, once a year, at the fête of the
bow.

X
Big Curly

I returned to Loisy; everyone was awake. Sylvie was all
dressed up, almost like a city girl. She called me up to her
room, ingenuous as ever. Her eyes still sparkled and her
smile was full of charm, but the pronounced arch of her
eyebrows gave her a serious look at times. Her room was
decorated simply, but the furniture was modern, the old
pier-glass having been replaced by a mirror in a gilded

---

[24]Gabrielle d'Estrées (1573-1599). Mistress of Henri IV and mother of the
ducal house of Vendôme. The reader is referred to the famous bare-
breasted portrait of Gabrielle and her sister in the bath.

frame, on which was painted an idyllic shepherd boy offering a bird's nest to a shepherdess in blue and pink. The four-poster draped chastely in old, flowered chintz had been replaced by a walnut bunk-bed with a draw-curtain; at the window, there were canaries in the cage where the warblers used to be. I hastened to leave that room, finding nothing there to remind me of the past. "Aren't you going to work on your lace at all today?" I asked Sylvie.

"Oh, I'm not making lace any more; there's no longer any demand for it in the area. Even the factory at Chantilly is closed."

"So what are you doing now?" She went to a corner of the room and brought back an iron instrument resembling an elongated pincers. "What's that?"

"It's what they call a *mécanique*; it's for holding glove-skins in place, so they can be sewn together."

"Ah, so you're a glovemaker, Sylvie?"

"Yes; we work here for Dammartin. The pay is very good these days. But today, I'm not working. Let's go somewhere, wherever you like." I glanced toward the road to Othys; she shook her head, and I understood that her great-aunt was no more. Sylvie called a little boy and had him saddle a donkey. "I'm still tired from yesterday," she said, "but an outing will do me good; let's go to Châalis." And off we went through the woods, followed by the little boy armed with a stick. Soon Sylvie wanted to stop, and I stole a kiss as we looked for a good place to sit down. Under the circumstances, conversation between us could not be very intimate. I had to tell her about my life in Paris, and about my travels.

"How could you go so far away?" she said.

"Now that I've seen you again, it amazes me that I could."

"That's easy to say!"

"And you must admit you're prettier now than you used to be."

"That's news to me."

"Do you remember when we were children together, and you were the taller?"

"And you the better-behaved?"

"Oh, Sylvie!"

"They used to put us both on the same donkey, one of us in each side basket."

"And we didn't say '*vous*' to each other then. . . Do you remember teaching me how to catch crayfish under the bridges on the Thève and the Nonette?"

"And you, do you remember your foster-brother,* who fished you out of the *warter** one day?"

"Big Curly! He was the one who had told me I could make it across the *warter!*"

I hastened to change the subject. These reminiscences had reminded me vividly of the time when I used to come to the country dressed in a little English-style suit that made the local people laugh. Only Sylvie thought me well-dressed; but I dared not remind her of that opinion she had held so long ago. For some reason or other, my thoughts turned to the wedding garments we had worn in her old aunt's house in Othys. I asked what had become of them. "Dear Auntie!" said Sylvie. "Two years ago at this time, she let me wear that dress to go dancing in, during carnival in Dammartin. She died the following year, poor dear!"

So much did she sigh and weep that I had no opportunity to ask how she happened to be going to a masquerade ball; but it was plain enough to me that thanks to her talents as

---

*Foster-brother (*frère de lait*): son of the woman who had wet-nursed the writer, when both were infants.

*Warter: a mispronunciation of "water," analogous to the French children's *ieau* for *eau*.

a seamstress, Sylvie was no longer a mere peasant girl. The other members of her family had remained in that condition, and she was living among them like an industrious, beneficent fairy, making life more abundant for them.

XI
Return

The scene came into view as we emerged from the forest. We had reached the shores of the Châalis ponds. The galleries of the cloister, the chapel with its soaring ogives, the feudal tower and the small castle where Henri IV and Gabrielle made love, all were tinged with the red glow of sunset against the dark green of the forest. "It's a Walter Scott landscape, isn't it?" said Sylvie.

"And who has been talking with you about Walter Scott?" said I. "You must have done a lot of reading in the past three years! . . . As for me, I am trying to forget all about books; what pleases me most is just being here with you, seeing once more this old abbey where, as little children, we used to hide from each other among the ruins. Sylvie, do you remember how frightened you were when the caretaker told us the story of the red monks?"

"Oh, that! Don't remind me!"

"Then sing me the song about the beautiful damsel abducted from her father's garden, beneath the white rose-tree."

"Nobody sings that any more."

"Have you by any chance become a serious musician?"

"I do a little singing."

"Sylvie, Sylvie! I'll bet you're singing operatic arias!"

"Why should you care if I am?"

"It's just that I like the old tunes, and you'll be forgetting how to sing them."

Sylvie modulated a few notes of a well-known aria from a modern opera. . . She was *phrasing*!

By this time we had reached and rounded the end of the first of the ponds. Here now was the greensward surrounded by lindens and elms, where we had so often danced together! I was vain enough to point out to her the old Carolingian walls, and to decipher the coat-of-arms of the House of Este. "Well, listen to you!" said Sylvie. "you've read a whole lot more than I have! So what are you, a scholar?"

I was piqued by her reproachful tone. I had been looking for the right moment to renew our expansive intimacy of the morning; but what could I say to her in the presence of a donkey and a very wide-awake little boy, who was enjoying himself by staying close to us, to hear the Parisian talk? At any rate, I made the mistake of mentioning the Châalis performance that I remembered so vividly. I led Sylvie into the very hall of the castle where I had heard Adrienne sing. "Now I'd love to hear *you* sing!" I said to her. "Let your dear voice ring out beneath these vaults and drive out that phantom that's been tormenting me, whether it be good or evil!"

Repeating the words after me, she sang:

> Angels, quickly now descend
> Into purgatory's depths!

"That's so very sad!" she said.

"It's just sublime. . . I think it's by Porpora,[25] with some

---

[25]Niccolò Porpora (1686-1766), Neapolitan composer. Henri Lemaitre: "Cf. George Sand's novel, *Consuelo* (1842)."

verses from a sixteenth-century translation."

"I wouldn't know," replied Sylvie.

We returned home via the valley, following the Charlepont road, which local people, having by nature little concern for etymology, insist on calling *Châllepont*. Sylvie, tired of the donkey, took my arm as we walked along. The road was deserted; I attempted to speak candidly of what was in my heart, but somehow I kept coming up with commonplace, banal expressions, or else with some flowery phrase from a novel—which Sylvie might have read. Finally I settled on a completely detached, impersonal style and tone, and from time to time she expressed surprise at my sporadic effusions. Upon reaching the walls of Saint S. . ., we had to watch our step carefully. There were soggy fields to be crossed, with rivulets winding through them.

"What's become of the nun?" I said suddenly.

"Oh! You're *terrible*! You and your nun! . . . Well, well! That remark has just spoiled everything."

Sylvie refused to say another word to me.

Can't women understand how a particular word can pass a man's lips, without coming from his heart? Apparently not; they are so easily deceived, and so often make the wrong choices. There are some men who play so well the subtle game of love! I have never been able to get the hang of it, even though I know that certain women deliberately allow themselves to be deceived. Besides, a love affair that dates back to childhood is something sacred. . . Sylvie, whom I had watched grow up, was like a sister to me. I couldn't try to seduce her. . . Then a totally unrelated thought crossed my mind. "At this hour," I said to myself, "I would be at the theater. . . So what is Aurélie (the actress's name) supposed to be playing tonight? Oh yes, the role of the princess in that new melodrama. That third act—how gripping it is! . . . And the love scene in the second act, with that wrinkle-faced juvenile lead!"

"Are you lost in thought?" said Sylvie; and she began to sing:

> In Dammartin there are three pretty girls,
> One of them as pretty as the day is long...

"Aha, naughty girl!" I cried. "It's plain to see that you *do* still know some of the old songs."

"If you came around more often, I could brush up on some," she said, "but we have to face reality. You have your affairs in Paris, and I have my work. Let's not be too late getting home; I have to be up with the sun tomorrow."

XII
Père Dodu

I was going to reply, to fall at her feet, to offer my uncle's house, which it was still possible for me to buy, since I was one of several heirs and that small property had not yet been divided up; but at that moment we arrived in Loisy. They were expecting us for supper. The patriarchal aroma of onion soup was spreading far and wide. Some neighbors had been invited in for this day-after-the-fête meal. I recognized immediately an old woodcutter name Père Dodu, who on winter evenings used to tell very funny or horrifying stories. Shepherd, messenger, gamekeeper, fisherman, even poacher, Père Dodu used to make cuckoo-clocks and roasting-jacks in his spare time. For a long time he had devoted himself to guiding English visitors around Ermenonville, taking them to Rousseau's various places of meditation while describing to them the great man's last days. It was he who had been the little boy whom the philosopher employed to sort his plant specimens, and to whom he gave the order to cut the hemlock whose sap he squeezed out into his *café au lait*. The innkeeper at the Croix d'Or used to dispute the latter claim; there were some lingering animosities over that. For a long time Père Dodu had been accused of possessing certain very innocent secrets, such as how to cure a sick cow by reciting a Bible verse backwards and making the sign of the cross with his left foot; but he had renounced all such superstitions early on, —thanks, he said, to some things he remembered Jean-Jacques' having said in his conversations.

"So it's you, little Parisian!" said Père Dodu to me. "You coming to seduce our girls?"

"Me, Père Dodu?"

"You leading them off into the woods while the wolf's away?"

"Père Dodu, it's you who are the wolf."

"I used to be, so long as there were ewes available; nowadays, all I can find are nanny-goats who know very well how to defend themselves! But you Parisians, you're such slick operators. Jean-Jacques was so right when he said: 'Man becomes corrupted in the poisoned air of cities.'"

"Père Dodu, you know all too well that man becomes corrupted everywhere."

Père Dodu struck up a drinking song; I tried in vain to stop him before he came to a certain scabrous verse that everyone knew by heart. Despite our entreaties, Sylvie refused to join in, saying that people didn't sing at the table any more. I had already noted that her Romeo of the previous night was sitting on her left. There was something about his round face and disheveled hair that was vaguely familiar to me. He got up and came over behind my chair, saying: "Don't you recognize me, Parisian?"

A woman who had been serving us, having just come back to the table for her dessert, whispered in my ear: "You don't recognize your foster-brother?"

Had it not been for this timely information, I would have

made quite a fool of myself. "Why—it's Big Curly!" I cried. "It's really you, the very lad who pulled me out of the *warter!*" Sylvie burst out laughing at this belated recognition.

"Not to mention," said the lad, embracing me, "that you had a beautiful silver watch, and that on the way home you were much more concerned about your watch than about yourself, for it had stopped running. You said, 'The *bug* is *drowned*, it doesn't go tick-tick any more. What will my uncle say?. . .'"

"A bug in a watch!" said Père Dodu. "So that's what they make children believe, down there in Paris!"

Sylvie looked sleepy; I supposed that in her view, I was a dead loss. A bit later, as I kissed her good-night at the door of her room, she said: "Come see us tomorrow!"

Père Dodu had remained at the table with Sylvain and my foster-brother; we sat and talked for a long while around a bottle of Louvres ratafia.* "All men are equal," said Père Dodu, between verses. "Here am I, drinking with a pastry-cook just as I might with a prince."

"Where's the pastry-cook?" I asked.

"Right there beside you! That ambitious young chap who is planning to set himself up in business."

My foster-brother looked embarrassed. By this time, I had begun to put two and two together. (Fate had reserved for me the irony of having a foster-brother here, in this region made famous by Rousseau—who had advocated the prohibition of wet-nursing!) Père Dodu informed me it was very likely that Sylvie would be marrying Big Curly, who was thinking of moving to Dammartin and opening a pastry-shop. That was enough for me. The Nanteuil-Haudoin coach took me back to Paris early the next day.

---

*Ratafia: a brandy-based liqueur flavored with almonds, fruit, etc.

XIII
Aurélie

To Paris! The coach takes five hours. I was in no hurry, having until evening to get there. By eight o'clock I was sitting in my accustomed seat; Aurélie expended her virtuosity and charm on some rather uninspired material from Schiller,[26] recently translated by a contemporary writer. In the garden scene, she was magnificent. During the fourth act, in which she did not appear, I went to Madame Prévost's and bought her a bouquet, inserting in it a very tender note signed, "An Unknown." "There!" I told myself. "That's something settled for the future." And the next day I was on my way to Germany.

What did I intend to do there? Try to sort out my feelings. —If I were writing a novel, I could never make the reader believe this story: a heart enamored of two women at the same time. I was losing Sylvie, through my own fault; but having been with her for just one day had been enough to cleanse and refresh my soul; from now on, I would keep her on a pedestal, like a smiling statue in the Temple of Wisdom. Her glance had stopped me when I was on the brink of the abyss. —I was more strongly repelled than ever by the thought of introducing myself to Aurélie in person, of figuring for a while among those tawdry Romeos who glittered and sparkled at her side momentarily and then fell away shattered and broken. "Some day we shall see," said I to myself, "whether that woman has a heart."

One morning I read in a newspaper that Aurélie was ill. I wrote to her from Salzburg in the Austrian mountains. My

---

[26]Material from Schiller's play. Henri Lemaitre: "...*Marie Stuart* by Pierre Lebrun, tragedy premiered in 1820, revived in 1840." Lemaitre suggests that by making Aurélie an actress of tragic depth, Nerval poetically "enlarges" Jenny Colon, whose *forte* was the operetta and light comedy.

letter was so steeped in Germanic mysticism that I could not have expected it to have much success with her, but then I did not sign my name nor request a reply; I counted on a little luck, and on the "Unknown."

Several months elapsed. During my wanderings and in moments of leisure, I had undertaken to put into the form of a poetic drama the story of the painter Colonna's love for the beautiful Laura, whose parents forced her to enter a convent, and whom he loved until death. Something about this subject seemed to relate to my own constant preoccupations. Once the last line of this play was written, all I could think of was returning to France.

What is there to say now that has not been said by so many others? I have jumped through all the hoops of those testing-grounds called theaters. "I have eaten drum and drunk cymbal," to quote the seemingly meaningless motto of the initiates of Eleusis[27] — which probably means that in case of need, one must be prepared to go beyond the limits of reason into nonsense and absurdity; my object in so doing was to define clearly my ideal woman and then to win her.

Aurélie had accepted the leading role in the play that I brought back from Germany. I shall never forget the day she permitted me to read the play with her. The love scenes had been prepared expressly for her. I believe I spoke my lines with feeling, but I'm certain I did so with enthusiasm. In our subsequent conversation I revealed myself as the "Unknown" of the two letters. She said to me: "You are quite mad; but do come to see me again. . . . I've never yet found anyone who knew how to love me."

---

[27]Eleusis, a city northwest of Athens, site of the Temple of Demeter, Goddess of the Corn, where the secret Eleusinian Mysteries were performed at harvest time in the Greco-Roman world. At some unknown date, Dionysus (Bacchus), God of the Vine, came to be worshipped in these rites along with Demeter (Ceres).

O woman! thou seekest love. . . And do I not also?

In the days that followed, I wrote to her what were probably the tenderest, most beautiful letters she had ever received; the ones I received from her were prosaic and non-committal. At last she weakened, called me to her, and confessed that she was finding it difficult to break off a previous attachment. "If you really love me *for myself,*" she said, "you will understand that I can belong to only one man."

Two months later I received an effusive letter of invitation, and I hastened at once to her lodgings. —In the meantime, someone had passed me a priceless bit of information: the handsome young man I had seen that night at the club had just enlisted in the Spahis.*

The following summer, there were horse-races at Chantilly, and Aurélie's theater troupe was at the disposal of its manager for three days. —I had become good friends with this fine man, a former Dorante in the Marivaux[28] comedies who had been playing juvenile leads for a long time in serious drama, and whose most recent success had been in the role of the lover in the play adapted from Schiller, in which my opera glass had revealed how wrinkled he was. At close range he looked younger; and since he had retained his slim figure, he still created quite a stir in the provinces. He had a great deal of spirit and drive. I accompanied the troupe in the capacity of "master poet"; I persuaded the manager to schedule performances in Senlis and Dammartin; he had at first preferred Compiègne, but Aurélie had sided with me. The next day, while arrangements were being made with theater owners and civil authorities, I hired some saddle-

---

*The Spahis: French cavalry units stationed in Algeria, famous for their showy uniforms.

[28]Pierre Carlet de Chamblain de Marivaux (1688-1763), novelist, and the most popular French dramatist of his time.

horses, and we rode out past the Commelle ponds to have lunch at Queen Blanche's castle. Aurélie, riding side-saddle with her blond hair flying, went galloping through the woods like a queen of the old days, and all the country folk, bedazzled, stopped to watch. —Except for Madame de F...,* they had never seen a woman so imposing in appearance and yet so gracious to everyone she encountered. —After lunch, we dismounted in some villages reminiscent of Switzerland, where the waters of the Nonette provide power for sawmills. These places, so dear to me in memory, interested Aurélie, but not enough to make her want to linger. As planned, I took her to the castle near Orry where I had seen Adrienne for the first time, on that open greensward. —She showed no emotion. Then I told her everything. I told her all about the beginnings of that great love of mine, at first dimly perceived by night, later dreamed about, and now at last fully realized in her. She listened to me attentively, and said: "You do not love me! You're expecting me to tell you that 'the actress is the same as the nun'; you're looking for a drama, that's all, and the dénouement escapes you. That's enough; I just don't believe you any more."

That speech was a thunderbolt. So those strange raptures I had been experiencing for so long, those dreams, those tears, those fits of despair and of tenderness. . . all that was *not love*? But then, what and where *is* love?

Aurélie performed that evening in Senlis. I thought I perceived in her a weakness for the troupe-manager—the wrinkled juvenile lead. He was a man of excellent character and had been of considerable service to her.

One day Aurélie said to me: "Now *there* is the man who loves me!"

---

*Madame de F. . .: Sophie Dawes, an English-born ex-harlot who as the Baronne de Feuchères made a very strong impression on the young Nerval with her flamboyant life-style.

XIV
Last Leaf

Such are the chimeras that bewitch and lead astray, in the morning of life. My attempt to characterize them has been somewhat haphazard, but many a heart will understand me. Illusions fall away one after the other, like the skin of a fruit, and the fruit itself is experience. Its taste is bitter; yet there is something strong and acerbic about it that fortifies —if I may be forgiven this antiquated phraseology. Rousseau says that the spectacle of Nature can be consolation for anything whatever. From time to time I go and revisit my own *bosquets de Clarens,** hidden away in the fog up there north of Paris; but everything there has changed so much!

Ermenonville! where the idyll of antiquity flourished anew—interpreted à la Gessner![29] You have lost your single star, which used to shine just for me with a dual luster. Blue and pink by turns, like the inconstant star Aldebaran, it was first Adrienne, then Sylvie, — the two halves of a single love. One was the sublime ideal, the other the sweet reality. What now to me are your shady paths, your lakes, even your wilderness? And you, poor neighboring hamlets of Othys, Montagny, Loisy and Châalis (now being restored)—there is nothing left in you of my past life! Sometimes I feel a need to behold again these places of my solitude and reverie. There I sadly discover within myself the ephemeral traces of a time when I affected a simplistic love of naturalness. I sometimes smile to read, chiseled in granite, certain verses by Roucher[30]

─────────────

*Bosquets de Clarens: a wooded area in Switzerland, immortalized by Rousseau in his writings.

[29]Salomon Gessner (1730-1788), Swiss pastoral poet and landscape painter whose prose work *Idyllen* (1756) presented nature in a highly idealized manner.

which once seemed to me sublime, —or some moralizing maxim above a fountain or grotto dedicated to the god Pan. The ponds, excavated at such great expense, are filled with useless, stagnant water that the swan disdains. Long gone is the time when the Condé hunts used to pass through here, their proud horsewomen riding side-saddle, their hunting-horns replying to each other and echoing afar! . . . To reach Ermenonville, there is no longer any direct route to be found. Sometimes I go via Creil and Senlis, sometimes via Dammartin.

It is always evening when I arrive in Dammartin, and I always spend the night at the *Image Saint-Jean*. They usually give me the same clean, tidy room with old tapestry on the walls and a pier-glass above the mirror. This room is a throwback to the era of bric-à-brac, which I have long since renounced. I sleep warm there, under the thick eiderdown commonly in use in this region. In the morning, when I open my window—which is framed by grapevines and roses—I have a delightful ten-league view to a green horizon, with poplar trees lined up in rows in all directions, like armies. Here and there a few small villages huddle beneath their pointed bell-towers, built, as they say in these parts, *en pointes d'ossements*.* One can see first Othys, then Eve, then Ver; Ermenonville would be visible beyond the forest, if it had a bell-tower; but in that philosophic enclave the church has been quite neglected. After having filled my lungs with the pure, bracing air one breathes on this high plateau, I proceed

---

[30]Jean-Antoine Roucher (1745-1794), pastoral poet. Author of *Les Mois* (The Months), modeled on James Thomson's *Seasons*. He was guillotined with André Chenier.

En pointes d'ossements (literally, "out of bone-splinters"): this may refer to the physical and economic hardships incurred by poor villagers who were obliged to build and maintain their own churches.

cheerfully downstairs and walk a short distance to the pastry-shop.

"Hey there, Big Curly!"

"Hey there, little Parisian!"

We punch each other amicably as we used to do when we were children; then I climb a certain staircase to where I am greeted by the joyous, welcoming cries of two children. Sylvie's Athenian smile lights up her happy face. I say to myself: "Perhaps that was the path to happiness, however,..."

Sometimes I call her Lolotte, and she thinks I look a little like Werther,[31] minus the pistols, which are no longer in vogue. While Big Curly is attending to lunch, we take the children for a stroll along the linden-shaded walkways which encircle the ruins of the castle's old brick towers. While the little ones are practicing archery like future bow-and-arrow club members, shooting their father's arrows into straw targets, we read aloud to each other some poetry or a few pages from those little books so seldom written any more.

I almost forgot to mention that on the day the troupe to which Aurélie belonged gave a performance in Dammartin, I took Sylvie to see the show, and I asked her if she didn't think that actress resembled a person she had once known.

"What person?"

"Do you remember Adrienne?"

She burst out laughing and said: "What an idea!" Then, as if reproaching herself, she added with a sigh: "Poor Adrienne! She died in the convent of Saint-S..., about 1832."

---

[31]Goethe's epistolary novel, *Die Leiden des jungen Werthers* (The Sorrows of Young Werther), is partly autobiographical, and depicts the unrequited love of the student Werther for Charlotte (Lolotte), the fiancée of his best friend. The publication of *Werther* in 1774 made Goethe world famous at twenty-five, and is said to have provoked a wave of suicides in emulation of its hero.

Chronology

Chronology

1807   Etienne Labrunie, of Agenese descent, marries Marie-Antoinette-Marguerite Laurent, a woman of Valois.

1808   *May 22.* Gérard Labrunie is born at No. 96, rue Saint-Martin, Paris.

1809   Doctor Labrunie, who in the preceding year had been appointed a junior medical officer in the Grand Army and then a senior medical officer in the Army of the Rhine, serves in Poland and Austria. His wife accompanies him. Gérard is left in the care of a wet-nurse at Loisy, near Mortefontaine.

1810   Doctor Labrunie becomes director of a military hospital at Hanover, then at Glogau, Poland. Marie-Antoinette Labrunie, aged 25, dies of a fever she contracted "from crossing a bridge loaded with corpses," according to Gérard. Gérard grows up at Mortefontaine, in the household of his maternal great-uncle Antoine Boucher. He will return there later during school vacations.

1812   *Napoleon's Russian Campaign.*

1814   Doctor Labrunie returns from abroad. Gérard is six years old.

1815   *Napoleon's Second Abdication. The Restoration.*

1820   Gérard is living with his father on rue Saint-Martin, Paris.

He is a pupil at the Lycée Charlemagne and has Théophile Gautier for a schoolmate. Uncle Antoine Boucher dies.

1826 Gérard (henceforth known as Gérard de Nerval) has his earliest works published by Touquet: *Elégies nationales* and *L'Académie ou les membres introuvables*. He is now 18.

1828 A much more serious work, a translation of Goethe's *Faust* which Gérard completed while living in Saint-Germain-en-Laye, is published by Dondey-Dupré. The poet's maternal grandmother dies. In this same year he is introduced to Victor Hugo.

1830 Premiere of *Hernani,* which Nerval attends. Publishes *Choix des poésies de Ronsard* and a translation of *Poésies allemandes*.

1830 *The July Revolution. The July Monarchy.*

1831 Dramatic essays *Le Prince des sots* and *Lara* staged at the Odéon. Gérard is arrested with some friends for disturbing the peace; spends a night in Sainte-Pélagie prison.

1832 Gérard is active in Jehan Duseigneur's "petit cénacle" and in "Jeune-France." Imprisoned in Sainte-Pélagie for the second time, as a result of the so-called Rue des Prouvaires Conspiracy. Cholera epidemic in Paris (Gérard a medical student at the time).

1833 Probably the year in which Gérard sees Jenny Colon for the first time; both are 25. Jenny is singing at the Variétés and will soon become somewhat famous.

1834 Gérard inherits 30,000 francs from his grandfather. Traveling in the south of France. First trip to Italy.

1835 In the Impasse du Doyenné, together with Théophile Gautier, Camille Rogier, Arsène Houssay et al., Gérard founds *Le Monde dramatique*, with a view to "launching" Jenny Colon.

1836   *Le Monde dramatique* is liquidated—a financial disaster. Heavily in debt, Gérard turns to journalism (*Le Figaro, La Charte de 1830*).

1837   Working on the staff of *La Presse*. Premiere showing of *Piquillo*. Love letters to Jenny Colon.

1838   April 11, Jenny Colon marries the flautist Leplus, ending her love affair with Gérard. First trip to Germany (Baden, Strasbourg, Karlsruhe, Mannheim, Frankfurt). From this trip comes the play *Léo Burchart*, accepted November 16 by Anténor Joly at the Renaissance.

1839   Premiere of *L'Alchimiste*, in collaboration with A. Dumas, at the Renaissance. *Léo Burchart* is eventually staged at the Porte Saint-Martin. Business trip to Austria (Lyon, Geneva, Bern, Zurich, Lindau, Munich, Salzburg, Linz, Vienna). In Vienna, Gérard meets Marie Pleyel and Liszt. Writes for Viennese journals.

1840   Returns to Paris. Prepares his translation of *Le Second Faust*. Trip to Belgium. Performance of *Piquillo* in Brussels, December 15. Meets with Jenny Colon-Leplus, through the intercession of Marie Pleyel, who is then in Brussels.

1841   Gérard's first mental crisis, February 21 or 23. He is taken to the house of Mme de Saint-Marcel, rue de Picpus; then, following another attack, to Dr. Esprit Blanche's clinic in Montmartre. Remains there until end of November. Meanwhile Jules Janin has written, in *Le Journal des Débats* of March 1, "the epitaph" of his mind and spirit.

1842   Jenny Colon dies, June 5. Gérard leaves for the Orient in December.

1843   Trip to the Orient: Marseilles, Malta, the Greek Islands, Egypt, Cairo, Alexandria, Lebanon, Beirut, Cyprus, Rhodes, Smyrna, Constantinople, Malta. Visit to Naples in late November. Return to Marseilles December 5.

1844   Putting in order his notes for *Voyage en Orient*. Trip to Holland and Belgium with Arsène Houssaye.

1845   A week in London.

1846   Excursions into Valois. Notes for *Angélique, Sylvie, Promenades et Souvenirs*.

1848   Gérard makes friends with Heine in Paris. Collaborates with him, translates some of his poems.

1849   *Les Monténégrins* performed at the Opéra Comique. New mental crisis in April; Gérard treated by Dr. Aussandon. Letters to T. Gautier describing the June 13 riot in Paris and the outbreak of cholera there. Trip to London.

1850   Stages *Le Chariot d'enfant* at the Odéon in collaboration with Méry. Period of depression; again treated by Dr. Aussandon. Trip to Germany.

1851   Negotiations with Charpentier for definitive edition of *Voyage en Orient*. Various projects for the theater. In September, another mental breakdown; goes to Dr. Emile Blanche in Passy. Premiere of *L'Imagier de Harlem* at the Porte Saint-Martin.

1851   *Coup d'état, December 1851.*

1852   *The Second Empire.*

1852   Gérard is hospitalized at the Maison Dubois (a municipal sanitarium). Trip to Holland in May. Negotiations with Giraud & Dagneau for *Lorely*. Work done for *Les Illuminés* appears in November. Excursion to Valois in August.

Material and mental difficulties.

1853   Preparatory work for *Sylvie*. Another sojourn in Maison
        Dubois. More excursions to Valois. *Sylvie* appears August
        15 in *La Revue des deux mondes*. New crisis August 25;
        Gérard taken to Hôpital de la Charité, then to Dr.
        Blanche's clinic. Checks out prematurely, suffers a re-
        lapse, returns to the clinic. At year's end, completes *Les
        Filles du feu* and *Les Chimères*.

1854   New project (deferred) for a trip to the Orient. Last trip to
        Germany, May to July. In August, Gérard goes back to Dr.
        Blanche's. Works on *Aurélia*. Leaves the clinic October 19
        to lead a wandering, homeless existence.

1855   January 26: Very cold weather in Paris (-1° F.). At dawn,
        Gérard is found dead in the Rue de la Vieille Lanterne,
        having evidently hanged himself.

(This chronology is based primarily on Raymond Jean's *Nerval
par lui-même*, Editions du Seuil: Paris, 1964)

Bibliography

Bibliography

Daumal, René. *L'Evidence Absurde: Essais et Notes, I (1926-1934)*. Edited by Claudio Rugafiori. Paris: Editions Gallimard, 1972.

Gautier, Théophile. *The Works of Théophile Gautier*. Vol. 8. Translated and edited by F. C. De Sumichrast. Boston and New York: C. T. Brainard Publishing Company, 1902.

Goncourt, Edmond and Jules de. *Pages from the Goncourt Journal*. Translated and edited by Robert Baldick. London, New York and Toronto: Oxford University Press, 1962.

Holmes, Richard. *Footsteps: Adventures of a Romantic Biographer*. New York: Penguin Books, 1986.

Houssaye, Arsène. *Man About Paris: The Confessions of Arsène Houssaye*. Translated and edited by Henry Knepler. New York: William Morrow and Company, 1970.

Jean, Raymond. *Nerval par lui-même*. Ecrivains de Toujours, no. 68. Paris: Editions du Seuil, 1964.

Knapp, Bettina L. *Gérard de Nerval: The Mystic's Dilemma*. Alabama: University of Alabama Press, 1980.

Nerval, Gérard de. *Œuvres*. Edited by Henri Lemaitre. Paris: Garnier Frères, 1966.

Nerval, Gérard de. *Œuvres complètes*. Vol. 2. Rev. ed. Edited by Jean Guillaume, Claude Pichois et al. Bibliothèque de la Pléiade. Paris: Editions Gallimard, 1984.

Nerval, Gérard de. *Selected Writings*. Translated and edited by Geoffrey Wagner. Ann Arbor: University of Michigan Press, 1970.

Poulet, Georges. *The Metamorphoses of the Circle*. Baltimore: The Johns Hopkins University Press, 1966.

Rhodes, S. A. *Gérard de Nerval 1808-1855: Poet, Traveler, Dreamer*. New York: Philosophical Library, 1951.

About the Translator

Born the only son of a school administrator in northwestern Ohio, Kendall Lappin evinced early on a strong affinity for the interplay of languages. After majoring in French and Spanish at DePauw University and achieving fluency in French at Middlebury College, he taught high school language courses (including English) in Fairfield, Illinois until the outbreak of World War II. Upon graduation from the Navy's Japanese Language School in 1944, he served as a junior officer in the Pacific theater. At war's end he was assigned to the U. S. Naval Academy, to teach foreign languages to the midshipmen; soon thereafter he converted to civilian faculty status and made Annapolis his career, adding (1954) a Middlebury M. A. degree in Russian to his qualifications. Since his retirement in 1976 he has been active in literary translation—mostly poetry—from French to English.